HIGH POCKETS

George Akers has no traditional love of the land. His real love is rodeo riding, and he only returns to the ranch his stepfather had driven him from to see that the old man is properly buried. The foreman tries to talk him into staying on to restore the fortunes of the Circle-A, but it is only when Ted Corbin, who holds a mortgage on the ranch, tries to force his hand that the stubborn George makes up his mind ... to stay and fight. Cathy Ballard might have something to do with it. So might her sister, Gay, a man-eating tramp. But maybe it's just that Akers is as mean as the rest, and no man is going to get the better of him, even if it means that someone has to die in the process ...

HIGH POCKETS

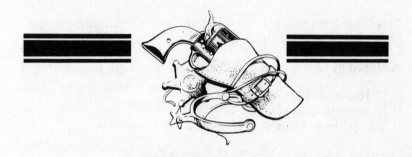

Herbert Shappiro

ATLANTIC LARGE PRINT
Chivers Press, Bath, England.
Curley Publishing, Inc.,
South Yarmouth, Mass., USA.

Library of Congress Cataloging-in-Publication Data

Arthur, Burt. 1899–1975
  High pockets / Herbert Shappiro.
    p. cm.—(Atlantic large print).
  ISBN 0–7927–1120–3 (lg. print : softcover).
  1. Large type books. I. Title.
[PS3501.R77H54. 1992].   91–38375
813′.52—dc20.   CIP

British Library Cataloguing in Publication Data available

This Large Print edition is published by Chivers Press, England, and Curley Publishing, Inc., U.S.A. 1992

Published by arrangement with Donald MacCampbell, Inc.

U.K. Hardback ISBN 0 7451 8381 6
U.K. Softback ISBN 0 7451 8393 X
U.S.A. Softback ISBN 0 7927 1120 3

FOR
MY WIFE

HIGH POCKETS

HIGH POCKETS

CHAPTER ONE

THE DEAD SLEEP UNHAPPILY

In a fenced-off clearing on the fringe of a grove of tall cottonwood trees, eleven men with bared, bowed heads stood looking down upon a freshly heaped grave. There was no movement among them, no sound ... suddenly, and startlingly, a man in the very middle of the solemn-faced group sneezed. Ten heads turned toward him and ten pairs of rebuking eyes glared at him ... he flushed and looked away. Standing on the opposite side of the mound was a tall, lean youth with steady, bitter eyes and a tightened mouth framed in a sun-bronzed face that was topped by a boyishly tousled head of blond hair. He towered above the other men. When he squared his shoulders and straightened up and hitched up his belt it was an indication that the simple service was over. The others raised their heads and waited again ... when he put on his hat, they clapped on their hats. There was an awkward, uncertain pause again, then the men facing him turned slowly, trudged off in a silent, shuffling body toward the bunkhouse beyond the corral. The tall youth did not move ... his thumbs hooked in his gun belt, he seemed to be far away in

1

thought. One or two of the trooping men looked back at him, exchanged glances with their companions; one man muttered something and shrugged his shoulder, then they went on again.

It was only when a slim girl appeared, seemingly out of nowhere, and stepped toward the grave that the bitter-eyed young fellow exhibited any interest. He looked at her and that look he gave her was more than just a passing glance. She knelt at the side of the mound and he saw her lips move in prayer. Presently she arose, turned away without a word or even a glance in his direction, and marched off. He followed her with his eyes ... there was another grave a short distance away and the look of surprise that flashed over his face indicated that he hadn't noticed it before. There was a wooden cross at the head of it ... the white paint on the cross gleamed brightly in the morning sunlight. The girl stopped beside it, knelt down. When she came erect a minute later, she turned her head and their eyes met. She came swinging across the intervening space with a springy stride, stopped in front of him, and looked up at him.

'I'm Cathy Ballard,' she said simply. She paused, evidently expecting him to say something in reply; when he did not answer, she went on. 'I'm terribly sorry about your father.'

2

'My stepfather, y'mean,' he said curtly.

She felt her cheeks crimson.

'Yes, I meant to say your stepfather,' she said. She saw his eyes range upward from her lips to her hair and she paused again ... his eyes came down to meet hers. 'He told me all about you. I think I'd have known you from his description of you even I had never seen those rodeo posters or heard someone say you were George Akers.'

His mouth seemed to tighten even more than before.

'What'd he know about me t' tell you?' he demanded. 'Or t' tell 'nybody else?'

She smiled fleetingly.

'O-h, lots of things,' she said brightly. 'For one thing, he knew all about your work with the rodeo. He was awf'lly proud of your reputation as a trick rider and expert roper. Then, whenever the show came within riding distance, he always went off to see you perform.'

He made no comment ... simply shifted his eyes away from her.

'He knew you were bitter,' she continued. 'Still, he always hoped that you'd forgive him somehow and that one day you'd come back and take over the Circle-A. That was all he lived for. I think he'd have died happily if he had known that you did come back after all.'

'You seem t' know lots about 'im,' he said. There was bitterness in his voice. She was

3

aware of it, however she pretended she hadn't noticed it. 'You two must've hit it off awright t'gether.'

'We did,' she said. 'He was like a father to me.'

'That's more'n he was t' me,' he answered. His eyes halted on the grave with the white cross above it. 'Who ... whose is that?'

'My father's.'

'Oh,' he said and it sounded more like a grunt.

'He was foreman of the Circle-A,' she explained. 'He was killed about four months ago.'

'Where are the rest o' your folks?'

'My mother died when I was a little girl. I've only a sister left now. She's married. She lives in Texas.'

'Where d'you live? Here? By y'self?'

'Yes ... in the cottage behind the big house. I've always lived there. I was born there.'

He was silent again.

'I suppose,' she continued presently. 'I suppose I should tell you that I'm going to be your first problem. Nettie Martin...'

'Who?'

'Phil Martin's wife.'

'Martin?' he repeated. 'Oh, yeah! He's the foreman, ain't he?'

'Yes.'

'Thought 'is name sounded f'miliar. What

4

was that you started t' say 'bout a problem?'

'We-ll, Nettie wants to move into the cottage.'

'And what are you supposed t' do?'

'Move out,' she answered. 'I don't want to. That's what makes it a problem, and you'll have to decide it. I admit Nettie's within her rights for after all her husband is foreman. Still, the cottage is home to me and that's why I've refused to give it up.'

'H'm,' he said. 'Where are they livin'?'

'In the big house.'

He turned his head, eyed her sharply.

'What's the matter with that?' he demanded. 'Ain't that good enough for th'm?'

'Of course it is,' she said quickly. 'It's just that Nettie wants her own place. I suppose every woman does.'

'Oh,' he said, and looked away again. 'Then maybe you oughta move out. Swap with th'm, I mean. Give them the cottage and move y'self into the house. It'll be better f'r you there. Livin' alone when you're young ain't the best thing in the world f'r yuh, b'lieve me. I know.'

'Very well. If that's the way you want it, that's the way it'll be.'

He turned to her again. There was a frown on his face. 'Wait a minute,' he said. 'Don't do it b'cause you think I want you to. It don't mean a danged thing t' me one way or another. I won't be around here long enough t' care a hoot who lives where, or even why.'

Her eyes widened with surprise.

'You mean you're . . .'

'This place may be home t' you,' he said coldly, interrupting her. 'It ain't t' me. Fact o' the matter is, the sooner I shake the dust o' the Circle-A offa my boots, the better I'm gonna like it.'

'But the Circle-A is yours now,' she said protestingly. 'You can't just leave it to itself and go off again. You can't . . .'

The frown became a scowl and she stopped abruptly, a bit breathlessly, too.

'I can't, eh?' he retorted. 'We-ll, I am. I don't know if Tex Akers ever told you, but he walloped all heck outta me one day, told me t' get off the place and to stay off. I don't hafta have a tree fall on me b'fore I get wise t' things. I got off the Circle-A and I stayed off, and if it wasn't f'r Judge Scott comin' after me and talkin' me into comin' back even if on'y f'r the funeral, I wouldn't be here now. We-ll, I've done the decent thing. Leastwise that's what the Judge called it. Now the funeral's over so I'm goin' back where I belong.'

'But . . .'

His lips thinned into a straight line.

'Look, sister,' he said curtly. 'I'm free, white and over twenty-one. I do 's I please and no buts about it. Get it?'

He hitched up his belt, a bit more viciously

than was necessary, turned on his heel and stalked off. He marched past the corral . . . he glanced at it mechanically as he passed it. There were a dozen horses idling within the barred enclosure and they seemed to sense that he was a stranger for they poked their heads through the bars and eyed him questioningly and appraisingly. One horse whinnied and the tall youth glared at him.

'Hey, George!' a voice called and the angry youth stopped and looked back over his shoulder. It was Phil Martin who had hailed him. 'Got a minute?'

'Yea, sure,' George replied.

The foreman, a pleasant-faced six-footer came striding up to him.

'I know this ain't the time t' start talkin' business,' Martin said apologetically. 'But there are a couple o' things that c'n stand 'tendin' to, so soon's you feel up to it, you holler f'r me, will you?'

'You'd better get hold o' Judge Scott. He c'n tell you what t' do.'

Martin looked surprised . . . finally he shrugged his shoulder.

'Whatever you say, George. You're the boss, y'know. I just figgered that since you're takin' over you'd . . .'

'I ain't takin' anything over. I'm leavin' here t'morrow.'

'Oh!' the foreman said for want of something better to say. 'I'm sure sorry about

7

Tex. I want you t' know that. He was a swell feller t' work for.'

'Who plugged 'im?'

'Nob'dy seems t' know f'r sure,' Martin replied. 'It could've been anyone of a dozen different fellers and with the exception o' one feller, they were all 'is friends.'

'Uh-huh. How'd it happen?'

'O-h, it was down in Corbin's place in town, y'know. Seems Tex was standin' at the bar when 'n argument come up and b'fore he could even get outta the way, all hell kinda busted loose. Most everybody in the place chipped in with some gunplay. Two fellers caught slugs in their shoulders, another feller got nicked on the jaw and Tex was sprawled out on the floor with a bullet right smack in 'is heart.'

'Corbin, did you say?'

'Yeah. Know 'im?'

'I know of 'im, and from what I've heard tell of 'im, he's bad medicine.'

'An' how! And what made th' hull thing stink t' high heaven was the fact that he and Tex weren't what you'd call chummy. Not by a jugfull either, b'lieve me! So soon's I heard about the shootin', I started puttin' two an' two t'gether t' get four. I got the answer awright, but how I got it, we-ll, that's somethin' else again.'

'Y'mean you kinda got the idea that maybe it wasn't an accident like it was supposed t' look, and that maybe Mister Corbin had more'n just a little somethin' t' do with it?'

Martin nodded grimly.

'You've been readin' my mail right over my shoulder, partner,' he said.

'Got 'nything to work on?'

'Nope. Nothing but the fact that Corbin had been pesterin' ol' Tex t' death, tryin' t' get him t' sell out.'

'And Tex wouldn't.'

'He finally wound up by tellin' Corbin t' get the hell offa the Circle-A and to stay off, and that come flood and high water, he'd still r'fuse t' sell the Circle-A.'

'What gave Corbin the idea that the Circle-A could be bought?'

'We-ll,' Martin began. 'The Circle-A ain't been the money-maker it had oughta be. This past year it's been tough goin' f'r the old man, tougher'n ever, I've been told. Understand rustlin' got pretty bad f'r a spell and cut deep into the herd. Then f'r some reason the water ran bad and that cost us a couple o' hundred head. Fin'lly, the bank started doggin' Tex f'r back interest and that kinda put the finishin' touches to things.'

'You figger that Corbin kinda got wind o' how things stood around here and that that was why he started workin' on Tex?'

'Uh-huh,' Martin said.

'Could be,' George said. 'On'y fr'm what I've been told about Corbin, he ain't the

9

ranchin' kind. Then why would he be after a spread that needs tendin' to all the time?'

'You got me,' the foreman said. 'Look, George...'

'Yeah?'

'We could do things with the Circle-A, you an' me. I know it. The ol' man's dead now and whatever he done t' you, we-ll, that's over with, buried with 'im. What d'you say George ... how 'bout givin' it a whirl, huh?'

'Nope. I don't want any part of it.'

'Yeah,' Martin breathed heavily. 'Still, I hate like hell t' see Corbin get 'is hands on it.'

'You better get hold o' Judge Scott,' George said. 'He prob'bly knows what's goin' on, so he oughta be the one t' tell you what t' do.'

There were a dozen men idling in front of the stagecoach station in the town of Shannon, Texas, when a pretty, young woman, colorfully yet tastefully attired, emerged from the hotel a short distance down the street. A dozen pairs of begrudgingly admiring eyes turned in her direction. Swiftly she marched to the waiting stage ... the driver who had been leaning against the rear wheel, came erect now. He touched the brim of his hat, opened the coach door, helped her mount the high step, closed the door behind her, then he swung himself up to the wide seat, unwound the reins from around the hand brake. He settled himself on the wide seat, released the brake and drove off. When the stage had rumbled around the corner, a tall man with a silver star pinned on his shirt front, sighed deeply, audibly.

'We-ll,' he said. 'That's that.'

There was a general nodding of heads.

'That's the end o' Gay Hollis,' he continued. 'Least ways, it's the end o' her far as Shannon's c'ncerned. Fr'm now on she's someb'dy else's headache, not ours. And f'r my dough, gettin' rid o' her is just about the best thing that's ever happened t' Shannon. Maybe now that she's gone, we c'n kinda go back t' livin' the way we used to, peaceable and quiet-like.'

Another man frowned deeply.

'Dave ain't even cold yet,' he said bitterly, 'and there she goes, flyin' 'er colors like 'n Indian, ridin' off t' hell knows where t' make trouble f'r some other unsuspectin' folks.'

'Where is she headed f'r?' a third man asked.

'How'n hell do I know?' the second man retorted. 'You know, Mike?'

'Understan' she's goin' to 'er sister's,' the lawman replied.

'An' where's 'er sister live?'

'She didn't say,' Mike said sharply. 'An' I wasn't interested enough t' ask.'

There was a brief silence.

'It sure is the doggonedest thing,' a man mused, 'how fifty men all s'pposed t' be in

11

their right senses c'n act like a lotta half-baked kids all on account o' one woman. Jerry, r'member what I said the first time I saw 'er?'

'Sure. You blinked at 'er like 'n goat wakin' up in a sunshiny day, swallered a couple o' times an' kinda wheezed, "Gee"!'

'You're a danged liar! Soon's I saw 'er, I said no good would come outta her, an' doggone if I didn't hit it right smack on the head. Half the men in town got one look at 'er and right then an' there they quit bein' good f'r anything but moonin'. Fr'm then on it was just a matter o' time when th' danged fools would f'rget that she was married t' Dave Hollis an' make a play f'r 'er right out in the open. S-ay, anybody seen Chris aroun' t'day?'

'Come t' think of it, I ain't.'

'He ain't been around,' Mike said briefly. 'He's gone.'

'What d'you mean ... he's gone?'

'Just what I say,' the law officer answered. 'He an' me had a talk last night after things quieted down. I suggested to 'im that he'd be a heap better off away fr'm Shannon, somewhere's where he could start all over again with nob'dy knowin' anything about 'im. He thought it over and fin'lly agreed that maybe it was a good idea. 'Course he didn't want 'nybody t' get the idea he was hightailin', even offered t' stand trial f'r killin' Dave if we wanted 'im to. I told 'im t'

12

quit bein' a damned fool an' made 'im get goin'.'

'It's gonna tak' 'im a long time t' get over this thing,' a man commented. 'He an' Dave were raised t'gether, y'know.'

''Course we know,' Mike said curtly. 'He wasn't no more responsible f'r what happened th'n Dave was. He was up in th' clouds somewheres when Dave stopped 'im and told 'im t' stay away fr'm Gay. He didn't even realize what was goin' on when Dave belted 'im. It was on'y when Dave went f'r 'is gun that Chris kinda come to. Even then all he tried t' do was take Dave's gun away when it went off. There wasn't nobody more s'rprised th'n Chris when Dave didn't get up. And when I grabbed 'im, he looked at me like he'd never seen me b'fore.'

'O-h, there ain't 'ny doubt that th' hull danged thing was accidental,' the man named Jerry said quickly. 'It's just tough that things had t' end up with a killin'.'

Mike hitched up his belt.

'We-ll,' he said with finality. 'Like I said b'fore, that's that. I dunno 'bout you fellers, but I got things t' do, so I'm gonna get goin'. See you later on.'

He turned and trudged away. The others separated . . . presently the stagecoach station was deserted. Peace and quiet had returned to Shannon.

13

CHAPTER TWO

MAN AND THE DEVIL

George Akers lay flat on his back on the bed in his room on the upper floor of the 'big' house. He stared moodily at the ceiling, raised his head when he heard the swift beat of an approaching horse's hoofs. He swung his long legs over the side of the bed, climbed to his feet and sauntered over to the window, whipped the curtain back and peered out. A horseman came swinging around the corral at a gallop, whirled onward toward the house ... a voice hailed him and he pulled up, twisted around in the saddle. Presently Phil Martin, a lariat slung over his shoulder, came striding up to him. There seemed to be little warmth in Martin's greeting ... actually it was nothing more than a curt nod. The two men talked briefly ... their conversation ended when Martin shrugged his shoulder and stepped back. The horseman loped off toward the house, rode past George's window, reined in near the back door and dismounted with the heavy awkwardness of a big man.

Cathy Ballard emerged from the cottage and started down the path that led to the house ... the newcomer looked up. Cathy

14

suddenly became aware of his presence, indicated it by stopping abruptly ... she seemed to be considering whether to go on or retrace her steps. After a moment she came on again. The man eyed her interestedly ... he stepped forward to meet her. George, watching from the window, saw her swerve toward the back door, saw the man intercept her and say something to her. Cathy flushed, pushed past him and went into the house. George frowned ... in another moment he was striding down the stairs. Cathy was standing near the kitchen table when he entered the room. She turned away quickly, busied herself at the dish closet. He was certain that her face was still flushed.

'Who's that feller outside?' he asked.

'That's Mister Corbin,' she answered over her shoulder.

'Oh,' he said. 'What's he want here?'

'You,' she said simply.

'You don't say! I saw him stop you and I kinda got the idea that he said somethin' t' you, somethin' you didn't like. 'Course I coulda been mistaken, y'know.'

'You weren't. I don't like anything Mister Corbin says.'

He was silent for a moment.

'How d'you know he's here t' see me?' he asked shortly.

'I'm sure he isn't here to see anyone else.'

'Then maybe I oughta go find out what he

15

wants.'

'It's a thought,' she said.

He went out the back way and the door slammed loudly behind him. Corbin, a tall, heavily-built man, was standing near his horse ... he seemed to be looking over the Circle-A with thoughtful and appraising interest.

'You lookin' f'r me?' George asked, stopping beside him.

Corbin turned quickly. He was a good looking man, with the flush of youth still in his face and a touch of gray in the hair at his temples.

'So you're George Akers!' he said with a smile. 'High Pockets himself, eh? I saw you do your stuff last year when the rodeo hit Plattsville. I've got to hand it to you, Akers. You did everything with that rope of yours except make it talk.'

'Thanks. That all you wanted t' see me about?'

'No, not quite,' Corbin said. 'I want to tell you that I'm mighty sorry about Tex's death. He was a good man.'

There was no comment from George.

'My principal purpose in coming here,' Corbin continued, 'was to talk with you about the ranch. I understand you're anxious to dispose of it.'

'You wanna buy it?'

'I do.'

16

'Why?'

'Why?' Corbin repeated in surprise. 'That's an odd question. Why would any man want to buy it?'

'To work it,' George answered calmly. 'But I can't see you doin' ranchin'. What d'you want the Circle-A for, huh?'

'Come, come, Akers. You're taking a strange attitude. Either you want to sell it, or you don't. Now which is it?'

'I'm plannin' t' sell it.'

'That's better.'

'But I won't sell it t' anybody 'cept a rancher.'

Corbin frowned, an indication that he was annoyed.

'What possible difference can it make to you who buys it?' he asked.

'Makes a heap o' difference t' me, Corbin. B'sides, I don't like t' do business with anybody I don't like.'

'I see,' Corbin said slowly. 'And I take it I'm to understand from that that you don't like me. Is that right?'

'Yep.'

Corbin's frown deepened.

'I don't know whether you've been told this or not...'

'Yeah?'

'I hold the mortgage on the Circle-A.'

'Awright ... I know it now.'

'Interest is due shortly. I take it you'll be

ready to pay it?'

'Come around and ask me when it's due.'

'I had hoped we'd be friends, Akers,' Corbin said. 'However, it appears you don't want any friendship.'

'That's just about the size of it.'

Cathy came out of the house and trudged up the path to the cottage. Corbin's eyes followed her.

'What'd you say t' her b'fore?' George asked.

'To her?'

'Yeah ... Cathy.'

'W-hy, nothing. That is, nothing of importance.'

'That's what I figgered. When she came into the house, her face was redder'n a beet. Mister, I understand Tex told you t' stay off the Circle-A. That goes double now.'

'For one who's supposed to want no part of...'

'You heard me!'

'Very well, Akers. But when a certain day comes, I'll...'

'Suppose we just wait f'r that day, huh?'

Corbin turned abruptly, swung himself up astride his horse, wheeled the animal.

'There's one thing more,' George said.

'Ye-es?'

'The next time you see Cathy, you might r'member t' kinda watch your tongue. If you don't, you're li'ble t' get y'self into a heap o' trouble. Savvy?'

Corbin's lips thinned. He pulled backward suddenly. The loose ends of the reins flashed upward and downward, almost in the same swift movement, and swished across George's face. The bitter-eyed youth staggered backward ... Corbin whirled his horse around, spurred him, sent him thundering away. George fell against the wall of the house ... someone caught him by the arms, steadied him, thrust a lariat into his hands. The tall youth gripped the coiled rope, broke away from Martin, stepped away from the house. He fumbled with the rope for a moment ... in another moment it sprang to life, spun in his hand, shot away with the awing speed of a darting snake. Corbin was some forty feet away when the pursuing noose overtook him ... it spun in a widening arc directly over his head, dropped like a flash, tightened around him. George braced himself on widespread legs, jerked his right arm backward and Corbin was lifted out of his saddle and hurled to the ground.

George tossed the rope aside, sprinted out to where the man lay outsprawled. Corbin rolled over, struggled to his knees, then to his feet ... he freed himself of the loose rope as George reached him.

'Why, you...!' he said through his teeth and swung viciously at the youth.

George sidestepped nimbly, pivoted and

smashed him fully in the face. It was a stunning and damaging blow ... it landed squarely on Corbin's nose with a curious, crunching sound and blood spurted from the man's nostrils. The fall had dazed Corbin ... the punch befuddled him. George swarmed over him, battered him with both hands, hammered him with pile-driving punches that sank wrist-deep into the man's body, then he whipped his fists upward to Corbin's jaw. It was a strange fight to watch ... Corbin, bloodied and battered, tried manfully to defend himself, to halt the plunging youth who seemed determined to batter him to the ground. But it was futile, and presently Corbin began to back up, tried to 'cover up' with his arms over his face and head. George simply shifted his attack and punched away at Corbin's body ... finally the older man broke. His arms came down, and George, on the alert, battered him half a dozen times in the face. Corbin stumbled away blindly, almost helplessly ... George gave no quarter. He pursued his opponent, straightened him up with a long, jolting left to the jaw. A group of wide-eyed men appeared, but they made no attempt to interfere. Corbin went down to his knees. A terrific, swishing punch that almost tore his head from his shoulders, lifted him off his knees ... winded, George stepped back and Corbin toppled over in a limp heap. The Circle-A punchers crowded around the panting youth. He pushed them away, hitched up his belt.

'Get him the hell outta here,' he breathed. ' He turned and trudged away toward the house. He tripped over the lariat and kicked it out of his way. Phil Martin, a broad grin of delight and satisfaction on his face, overtook him, glanced at him, stepped ahead of him when they reached the house, yanked the kitchen door open, held it wide, and followed George inside. Cathy came in at their very heels. She brushed past Phil, stepped around George, stopped directly in front of the tall youth and looked up at him with probing, anxious eyes.

'H'm,' she said, stepped back and rolled up her sleeves. 'Sit down.'

George eyed her belligerently, but she disregarded it. She reached for the nearest chair, gripped it and swung it around with surprising ease.

'Sit down,' she said a second time.

George obeyed. She snatched a towel off the rack that jutted out from the wall, whipped it open, draped it around George's neck without a word, tucked the ends into the open collarband of his shirt. Quickly and deftly she filled a basin with water from a huge pitcher, reached for a bottle on the top shelf of the dish closet ... George followed her every movement with his quiet eyes, watched her pour some of the bottle's

21

contents into the basin. She stopped in front of him again presently, an indication that she was finally ready for him.

'This will smart,' she said. 'However, as long as you were able to stand up and fight back after getting your face lashed, you should be able to stand this.'

George did not answer. Martin, tongue in cheek, watched the proceedings for another minute, then he backed very quietly to the door, opened it noiselessly and slipped out. He was grinning again when he strode away toward the corral.

★   ★   ★

It was an hour or two later. George, feeling considerably annoyed with things, particularly with himself, and unable to smell anything but the cleansing vinegar that Cathy had used on him so liberally, was straddling an up-ended box near the corral when the rumble of approaching wagon wheels filled the air. He turned his head ... a wagon drawn by two galloping horses came whirling around the corral, took the turn toward the house on just two wheels, flashed past him and pulled up presently almost within reach of the back door. He had caught a fleeting glimpse of the wagon's occupants, a bemustached man with a scowling face and a pretty young woman. He turned his head, saw them alight. In another moment the wagon rumbled off again. Cathy came out of the house ... she cried out delightedly, caught the young woman in her arms, and hugged her. For another moment the two talked excitedly, then they turned and went inside.

It was probably half an hour later when George mounted the stairs to the upper floor, turned toward his room ... he stopped abruptly and raised his head. Framed in the open doorway of the room directly opposite his own room was the pretty, young woman who had arrived earlier. She was smiling at him. She was the prettiest woman he had ever seen.

'Hello,' she said brightly.

'Huh?' he said. 'O-h, h'llo.'

She sniffed suddenly.

'Vinegar!' she exclaimed and made a wry face. 'It ... it's awful, isn't it?'

'Yeah, reckon it is,' he answered sheepishly and colored. 'Got the doggoned thing all over me, too.'

'Oh!' she said quickly. 'That's why the smell grew stronger. It was you coming upstairs.'

He frowned, turned toward his door.

'You're ... you're George, aren't you?' she asked. 'George Akers?'

'That's right,' he said over his shoulder.

'I'd have known you anywhere,' she went

23

on, then she laughed softly. 'Of course the vinegar might have fooled me, but not for long. I'm Gay Hollis.'

'Gay . . .'

'Yes. I'm Cathy's sister,' she added.

'Oh, yeah. Seems t' me Cathy did say somethin' about havin' a sister. I think she said you were livin' in Texas.'

'I don't live there any more.'

'Moved, eh?'

'We-ll, yes. You see, I've lost my husband, and now that I'm all alone, I've decided my rightful place is here with Cathy. She needs someone to look after her, you know.'

He nodded . . . however his thoughts went back to the scene in the kitchen and to Cathy's vinegar treatment.

'She seems t' know how t' do things awright. I'll say that for 'er.'

'I suppose I should have written both you and her before I left Texas,' Gay went on. 'But I was so terribly overcome when Dave died, we-ll, I simply had to get away from things without delay. Those memories . . .'

'Sure,' he said quickly. He thought he had detected a slight quivering of her chin and a catch in her voice and he was afraid she was going to burst into tears. 'Sure. I c'n understand.'

'Then . . . then you aren't angry with me for simply moving in on you without warning?' she asked almost timidly.

24

''Course not,' he said assuringly. 'This house is bigger'n a barn. Got plenty o' room here f'r you and then some. Cathy's supposed t' move outta the cottage so you two oughta be able 't fix y'selves up right comf'table in here. You just make y'self 't home and if you don't see what you want, just holler f'r it and you'll get it.'

She smiled up at him brightly again ... there were tears in her eyes.

'Thank you,' she said simply.

'Heck,' he said with an embarrassed grin. 'Forget it.'

His eyes fell before hers ... he turned away quickly, awkwardly, and went into his own room. The door closed behind him and in that instant Gay's tears vanished. She smiled a strange smile, stepped back inside and closed her door.

*   *   *

When Phil and Nettie Martin came to the Circle-A, Phil to take over the duties of ranch foreman, and Nettie to make a home for them there, there was a handful of punchers idling in front of the bunkhouse. The men looked up interestedly when the heavily-laden Martin wagon carrying all of the couple's wordly goods rumbled around the corral and braked to a stop in front of the 'big' house. The men had been told about Phil; they glanced at him appraisingly, then their eyes shifted as one to Mrs. Martin.

'Not bad,' one man said as he spat out a mouthful of tobacco juice.

'O-h, I dunno,' another man answered after a full minute's deliberation and study of the lady in question. 'She's awright, I suppose, if you like 'em lean. Me, I've allus had a likin' for the meaty kind. 'Course every man's got his own ideas about women, and that's the way it should be. It'd sure be one helluva mess if everybody liked the same kind, wouldn't it? What would we do with the left-overs ... y'know, the ones nob'dy wanted?'

Nettie was thirty ... Phil was twenty-seven. She had known him for more than ten years when he asked her to marry him. Womanlike, Nettie asked for time to think it over, although her answer was on the tip of her tongue even before he came to the end of his stumbling, awkwardly worded proposal. Nettie knew it would never do to accept him at once ... accordingly she waited an hour, then she strode briskly up to Phil's cabin and called him out, smiled at him when he emerged, stepped up to him, kissed him on the cheek and blushed fittingly. Actually, that was all there was to it. Shortly after, they drove in Phil's wagon to a neighboring town, routed an old Judge out his bed, and were married. Phil blushed and stammered in his answers, but Nettie was calm and collected, as though marriage ceremonies were every day happenings in her life.

They drove back to Phil's cabin, pulled up in front of it and climbed down. Nettie, stepping ahead of Phil, opened the door and poked her head inside. She shook her head, took off her wedding hat and handed it to her rather surprised husband.

'Go sit in the wagon,' she said and rolled up the full sleeves of her dress.

He stared at her wide-eyed, backed away ... finally he shrugged his shoulder, climbed up on the wide driver's seat and seated himself there with his long legs dangling over the side. From time to time he looked down at the frilly hat in his hand and shook his head. Nettie had disappeared inside the cabin, pulled the door shut behind her ... he wondered what she was doing in there. An hour later she opened the door.

'All right,' she called from the doorway. She smiled and rolled down her sleeves, added a smoothening pat to the front of her dress. 'You can come in now.'

Phil obeyed. The cabin was so orderly, it made him feel uncomfortably strange, almost like an intruder. The cabin stayed orderly, and in the days that followed his respect and admiration for Nettie grew. There was no lost motion in anything she did ... she was direct, practical and thoroughly capable. Nettie did something else for her youthful husband. Marriage to her was a permanent affair ... accordingly she took things into her own hands to insure her future, her children's, and of course, her husband's. Nettie took everything into consideration, and that accounts for her thoughts of children. There was no questioning the fact that she expected to have them ... she would decide when and how many.

'Phil,' she said one morning at breakfast. 'I want you to get yourself another job.'

'Huh?' he asked in surprise. 'What's the matter with the one I've got?'

'There's no future in it,' she said simply.

'O-h, I dunno.'

'We-ll, I do,' she said with finality.

He shrugged his shoulder.

'Awright,' he said. 'What d'you want me to do?'

'A man's best chance lays in ranching,' she explained. 'I think Tex Akers could be approached properly. He needs a foreman.'

'Uh-huh. And you think maybe he'd c'nsider me?'

'He'll do more than that when we get finished talking with him.'

'We?'

'I'm going with you, of course. Get the wagon while I clear these things away.'

Tex Akers went to his grave believing that it was he who had hired Phil Martin to serve as his foreman ... actually their conversation was but a few minutes old when Nettie took command of it.

'Phil has a lot to offer an employer who knows his business,' she said with a disarming smile. 'That's why we selected you as the man to talk to, Mr. Akers.'

'We-ll, thanks,' Tex said and laughed.

'You're a respected member of this county.' Nettie continued. 'Then too the people who've worked for you speak well of you, and that's always a good thing to know about a man. You've got a good ranch here, and with a strong, trustworthy young man to shoulder some of your duties and responsibilities, I think the Circle-A should do even better than before. Finally, Mr. Akers, Phil is a lot like you and that's all the more reason why I want him to work for you.'

'We-ll, now ...'

'Phil will be satisfied with a starting wage of a hundred and fifty a month. Of course, later on, when he's gotten the hang of things around here, you and he can talk it over and work out something that'll be satisfactory to both of you.'

Tex gulped and swallowed hard. He had paid Dan Ballard a hundred and ten dollars a month ... forty a month more was something to consider. Under normal conditions there would have been time for consideration ... Nettie had other ideas and none of them

29

allowed for loss of time.

'We'll be here early Monday morning,' Nettie said smoothly. 'Goodbye, Mr. Akers. I'm sure we're going to like it here.'

That was how Phil Martin came to work for the Circle-A. Now it was many months later. Tex Akers was dead, buried, and in his place as owner was lanky George Akers. Nettie was standing midway between the cottage and the 'big' house. There was a warm glow of satisfaction within Nettie ... Cathy was finally vacating the cottage in favor of Nettie and Phil. As Nettie waited, Cathy, her arms filled with things that ranged from dresses to pots and pans, came out of the cottage, sailed past Nettie without so much as a glance in her direction, stalked down the path and swept into the house. A minute later George Akers sauntered out. Nettie had already decided that it was about time that she and her husband's new employer talked things over. She squared her slender shoulders and started toward him at her usual brisk pace, stopped abruptly when Gay Hollis came out of the house. Nettie eyed her and frowned. Her frown deepened when she saw Gay overtake George and stop him. As Nettie watched, they talked and laughed. Perhaps it was womanly intuition or instinct ... whatever it was, Nettie instantly decided that Gay Hollis was just another way for spelling trouble. When Phil came striding up to them from the corral, Nettie's thoughts were troubled. They talked for a minute, then the three of them strolled off. Nettie turned away slowly.

CHAPTER THREE

TROUBLE RIDES A HORSE

It was the morning after the Martins had moved into the cottage. It was just after six o'clock when Phil came downstairs to breakfast. His face glowed, proof that he had scrubbed it; his hair was wet and slicked back. He smoothed down his shirt front, halted in the kitchen doorway.

'Hi,' he said.

Nettie was busy at the small stove.

'Good morning, Phil,' she said without turning.

He came striding over to her, bent and kissed her on the neck.

'Phil!' she said.

He kissed her again, louder, and on the same spot.

'Phil!' she said again. 'You know I don't like that. It ... it tickles. I nearly dropped this pan of batter.'

'Heck,' he said and turned away. He lifted the half curtain over the kitchen window, peered out, sniffed and turned around again. 'Boy, that coffee sure smells good. I could even smell it upstairs. Bet that's what woke me up. S-ay, what's that batter stuff for, huh?'

'Biscuits,' she said over her shoulder.

'Oh, yeah? Swell!' He swung a chair away from the table, seated himself, tilted the chair back on its rear legs. 'What time did you get to bed last night?'

'It was rather late,' she admitted.

'It must've been doggoned late! Here it is the morning after we move into this place and you've got it all fixed up a'ready. Curtains up, dishes in the closets. I gotta hand it to you, Nettie. S-ay, them biscuits gonna take long? My belly feels like...'

'Your stomach.'

'Huh? O-h! Awright then, my stomach feels like my throat's been cut.'

'They'll be ready in a jiffy.'

He moved his chair closer to the table as she placed a platter of bacon before him, followed it with a cup of coffee. She watched him for awhile, smiled as he emptied the cup. She filled the cup, then set a plate of steaming hot biscuits on the table.

'Boy!' he said. 'Boy!'

Nettie did not eat with him ... she preferred to serve him, and she enjoyed watching him do away with the things she placed before him. Three times she filled his coffee cup. Finally he sat upright again. He shook his head.

'We're gonna hafta cut this out, Nettie,' he said gravely.

'Nonsense!'

'We-ll, first thing y'know I'm gonna get so danged fat, my horse ain't gonna be able to carry me aroun'. Fr'm now on I'm gonna eat 'bout half o' what I've been puttin' away.'

'Then you don't want me to bake that layer cake tonight?'

His eyes widened.

'Layer cake?' he repeated. 'Choc'lit?'

'Yes.'

He frowned, rubbed his chin with his right thumb reflectively.

'I suppose it'd still be awright if I started cuttin' down on things t'morrow, wouldn't it, 'stead o' t'night . . . huh?'

'I think it would be all right.'

He grinned, climbed to his feet. He looked about him for a moment.

'You see that hat o' mine?'

'You might try that closet off the kitchen.'

He strode out of the room, returned presently, his hat in his hand.

'That's where it will always be,' she said: 'That is, when you aren't wearing it.'

He pinched her cheek playfully, marched to the door. She followed at his heels. He put on his hat, hitched up his belt, opened the door, turned to her again.

'See you later,' he said, bent to kiss her. She raised her head. Out of the corner of her eye she saw a slim figure emerge from the big house. It was Gay. Phil straightened up. 'Now what d'you suppose she's doin' up so early?'

He went striding out, swung down the path ... Gay heard his step; she turned and waved to him.

'Good morning,' she called.

'Mornin',' he answered and touched his hat. 'Kinda early f'r you to be up and doin', ain't it?'

'I like to ride early,' Nettie heard her say.

'In that case,' Phil said, stopping beside her. 'Come on along with me. Let's see what we c'n line up for you down at the corral. Oughta have somethin' that rides easy.'

Nettie, still framed in the cottage doorway, saw them walk off. A couple of punchers came out of the bunkhouse, followed them in the direction of the corral. Nettie closed the door slowly. She made her way to the table, sank down into the very chair that Phil had been using but minutes before. She sat upright again and listened when she heard a shout, the pounding of hoofs, and then a lingering scream. She got to her feet and went back to the door, opened it and peered out. A plunging horse with a screaming girl astride him came whirling into view. Nettie caught her breath. Men appeared suddenly, almost

34

from all directions ... they ran toward the approaching careening horse, shouted and gesticulated. The horse veered away from them, darted past them and headed for the open range beyond the ranch.

Nettie went flying down the path, swerved away from the house, raced past it and panted into the open ... a horseman bent low over his mount's neck thundered past her. It was Phil. She raised her head ... she wanted to call to him, to warn him to be careful but he was gone before she could give voice to her cry. Other mounted men thundered by in pursuit. Then Nettie saw some of them pull up in a skidding, dust-raising stop ... her eyes widened. There was Phil riding back, surrounded by a group of punchers ... in his arms and clinging to him, her head down and pressed against his chest, was Gay Hollis. Men ran up to them and Phil's horse stopped. Arms were thrust up for Gay. She straightened up, suddenly threw her arms around Phil's neck, drew his head down and kissed him soundly, squarely on the mouth. Phil blushed and laughed to cover up his embarrassment. Gay released him, turned and slid down, into the arms of a waiting cowpuncher who caught her lightly, grinned and set her down on the ground. Phil dismounted, busied himself tightening his mount's cinches. Nettie went back to the cottage.

It was nearly sundown when Phil came trudging up the path to the cottage. Nettie heard his heavy step, but her thoughts appeared to be elsewhere at the moment. He opened the door, poked his head in . . . Nettie was setting the table.

'Hi,' he said.

Nettie looked up.

'Oh!' she answered. 'Hello.'

She noted in that quick upward glance that he was drawn and tired, noticed too that he seemed unusually dirtied. He closed the door with a backward thrust of his right foot, came over to her, bent to kiss her . . . she turned her head and he kissed her cheek. He took off his hat, sailed it across the room . . . it landed on a chair, caromed off and whirled away. He moved past Nettie, leaned against the dish closet.

'Gosh,' he said. 'I'm plumb wore out.'

There was no response from Nettie.

'Been ridin' the fences all day,' he continued. 'That's the doggonedest job. Ridin', climbin' down, bendin' over, tightenin' or testin', then ridin' on and goin' through the same things every couple o' hundred feet. My back's near busted. Gotta talk to George 'bout them fences. Oughta have one feller to do nothing but take care o' th'm. S-ay, he's still around, ain't he?'

'George?'

'Uh-huh.'

'He was this afternoon,' Nettie answered without looking up.

'Then he ain't hightailed it like he said he was gonna do,' Phil mused.

'Perhaps he's found something to keep him here.'

'Huh? What d'you mean?'

'We-ll, every time I saw him, that Hollis woman was with him.'

'O-h, you mean Cathy's sister?'

'Of course.'

'Aw, that don't mean 'nything. 'Less I got him figgered out all wrong, George don't go f'r women.'

Nettie looked at him over her shoulder. 'I've yet to meet the man who doesn't,' she said coldly. 'Especially where women like that Hollis woman are concerned.'

'Heck,' he said and laughed. 'Doggoned good thing you didn't see what happened this mornin'. You'd be gettin' ideas about me, too.'

'I did see it,' she said quietly.

'You did?'

'Yes.'

He eyed her oddly for a moment.

'O-h,' he said. 'So that's what's bitin' you.'

He stepped to her side again, caught her in his arms. She struggled to free herself, held him off at arm's length.

'Phil ... please!'

'On'y wanted to kiss you, y'know.'

37

Her face was strangely, unexplainably flushed. She sniffed and backed away from him.

'You ... you smell of horses!'

The expression of hurt, and surprise, went out of his eyes.

'Yeah,' he admitted a bit lamely. 'Reckon I do.'

'Why don't you go upstairs and get cleaned up?' she suggested. 'Supper isn't quite ready yet.'

'That's 'n idea,' he said. He hitched up his belt. 'I won't be long. But if you're ready b'fore I'm done, just holler, will you?'

There was little conversation at supper, and even less while Nettie cleared away the table and washed the dishes. Phil was tired. He swung his chair away from the table and stretched his long legs. He sighed, closed his eyes. Minutes later he was asleep. It was nine o'clock when Nettie bent over him, shook him gently.

'Phil.'

There was no response, and she shook him again.

'Phil.'

He stirred, raised his head, slowly opened his eyes.

'Huh? S'matter?'

'The bed's open. Why don't you go upstairs and turn in?'

He yawned, covered his gaping mouth with

38

a big hand, stretched himself.

'Yeah, maybe I oughta. I'm so doggoned tired, I could sleep f'r a week,' he said. He scratched his head, rubbed his nose . . . he climbed to his feet, yawned again. 'How 'bout you? Ain't you gonna turn in too?'

'Not just yet. I've got some darning to do, then I'll be up.'

'Not like last night, y'hear?'

He turned and trudged out of the room . . . she followed him with her eyes, until he disappeared on the stairs. Presently she heard him overhead.

'Nettie!' he called.

'Yes? What is it?'

'I ain't gonna go t' sleep 'till you come up,' he went on. 'I'm just gonna lay here. So you better hustle it up.'

She did not answer.

It was after ten when Nettie went upstairs for the night. As she turned into the landing she heard Phil's heavy breathing. Rays of yellow lamp light streamed into the passageway from the open bedroom door. She peered into the room . . . Phil lay on his side, his back to the door. She tiptoed around the bed, stopped for a moment to lower the wick in the lamp that stood on the bureau against the far wall. Noiselessly she opened the closet door . . . her night clothes hung on the first hook. She lifted them off, slipped them over her arm, retraced her steps, stopping again when she reached the bureau to turn out the light. She undressed in the darkness, made her way to the bed and got in. The sheets were cold and she huddled beneath the blankets. Phil stirred ... suddenly he rolled over. His left arm, weighty as an oak when he was asleep, came around her, imprisoning her. She lay very still, almost at the very edge of the bed, breathing with an effort, and tempted to push his arm away.

But he was warm, and presently the warmth of his body reached her and she was more comfortable. She closed her eyes. Instantly her mind was filled with disturbing faces and scenes. In all of them Gay Hollis' face appeared. Her eager, dancing eyes seemed to be seeking someone ... her warm, tempting lips parted for a moment, puckered and swept downward, swerving past Nettie to reach Phil's. Nettie tried to drive the vision out of her thoughts. She was jealous and she was angry, first with Phil for despite the fact that he had been an innocent party to the kissing, his participation in it brought him within the range of Nettie's anger. She was angry with herself, too ... she hadn't meant to let Phil know how she felt about it, and now that he knew, she was miserable. He stirred again, moved a bit closer to her. He smelled of soap, but it was a clean smell and she offered no objection.

Then suddenly she was no longer angry

with him. Instead she was sorry she had been so cold and curt to him, sorry too for herself. She wanted to cry but there was no point in crying with him asleep and without him to comfort her. She slid down so that her head rested against his shoulder. When he turned over on his back, her head moved into the hollow of his arm. Her arm crept around him, tightened around him emotionally. When he moved his arm, he brought her head onto his chest. She sighed inwardly, deeply and contentedly, and closed her eyes. Now there were no disturbing thoughts. Gay Hollis' face did not reappear. Presently Nettie's gentle breathing indicated that she was asleep.

Cathy was tired. It had been a full day for her. Moving into the big house had brought her added responsibilities and duties ... quite naturally she took over Nettie's work as housekeeper and cook. This day she had rearranged the room she and Gay were sharing; she had washed the window, washed, ironed and hung the curtain for their window, put Gay's things away, and then her own, and now, at eleven, she was preparing for bed. Her nightgown on, she drew back the blankets, got into bed, looked over at Gay who was sitting at the window.

'Going to sit there all night?' Cathy asked. 'It's eleven o'clock, you know.'

Gay turned in her chair.

'I'm not tired,' she answered lightly. 'Want

41

me to turn out the light?'

'Do you mind?'

'Not at all. Actually, I like to sit in the darkness. It's restful.'

Gay moved swiftly. Presently the room was plunged in darkness. Cathy burrowed deep into the blankets, sighed so contentedly that Gay laughed.

'Comfortable?' she asked.

'Oh, yes! Bed's a wonderful place, isn't it?'

'Very wonderful,' Gay replied. She moved the curtain aside and rays of silvery night light streamed into the window. 'The light's out in the cottage.'

'Phil has to be up early. That's part of a foreman's job.'

'He's nice, isn't he?'

'Yes, he is.'

'What's his wife like? I haven't had more than a glimpse of her.'

'O-h, Nettie's all right, I suppose. We haven't gotten along as well as we should, still I don't know that it's been all her fault. I was pretty nasty with her over the cottage, you know. However, it's hers now, so I suppose we'll get along lots better.'

'She's older than Phil, isn't she?'

'Nettie? Do you think so?'

'Oh, yes!' Gay said. 'I'm sure she is.'

'I guess I've never given that matter any thought. What do you think of George?'

'I don't know what to think of him. He

isn't the talkative kind. Still I suppose he's all right. He's just not my kind of man. That's all.'

'I like him. I admit he's different than most other men but that may be why I like him. Anyway, he's had a hard time of it and I think it's made him quiet, even bitter.'

'I'll take Phil Martin's kind any time.'

'Nettie might not like to hear you say that.'

'When a plain, unattractive woman marries a man who is younger than she is, we-ll, she should expect most anything. I never could understand such marriages. They ... they don't make sense.'

There was no reply from Cathy. Gay settled herself in her chair. Cathy turned over on her side, and closed her eyes. She was tired, but sleep did not come easily. Gay's remark rang in her ears and it disturbed her. She wondered what kind of married life Gay had had. She'd said but little about it since her arrival, even less about her husband other than a brief word or two about his death.

'Gay.'

'Yes?'

'What sort of man was Dave?'

'You met him. Don't you remember?'

'I recall that he was tall and good looking.'

There was no comment from Gay.

'Why did that man shoot him?' Cathy asked.

'They ... they quarreled,' Gay answered

43

and it struck Cathy that her explanation seemed strangely hollow. It puzzled Cathy. 'Don't you think you ought to go to sleep now?'

'Did they ... quarrel over you?' Cathy pressed.

Gay was silent.

'They did, didn't they?'

Gay bounded to her feet.

'If you must know,' she said in icy tones. 'Yes!'

'Oh!' Cathy said, startled and taken back. 'I'm sorry. I shouldn't have pressed you so.'

'You wanted to know what kind of a man Dave was,' Gay went on wildly. 'All right ... I'll tell you!'

'Gay, please ... you'll wake George. He's just across the hall, you know.'

'I don't care! Let him hear me. Let the whole world hear me!' Gay exclaimed. She paused and drew a deep breath. It was a curious, animal-like, sucking sound. 'Dave's spread was a small one, but not because he couldn't afford to buy a bigger one, or buy more land to add to what he had. He wanted a small place because then he could work it by himself. Expanding or buying a bigger place meant that he'd have had to hire some help, and he didn't want any other man around the place.'

'I see.'

'The nearest town to us was Shannon, and

that was about twenty miles away. I never went there. Dave wouldn't let me. When we needed anything from town, Dave went for it while I stayed at home. He couldn't understand why I should want to get away from home once in a while, too, to see things, to meet other people, to talk to someone else for a change. Why couldn't I have been contented? Wasn't it a wife's duty to be contented? You'll never know, Cathy, how miserable I was, and how little he understood me.'

'I can see that.'

'Then he began to call me an ingrate. He felt I should be grateful for the roof over my head, for the bed I was permitted to sleep in, and for the food I was allowed to eat.'

'Oh, Gay!' Cathy said incredulously.

'He had very little time for me. He worked every day in the week, from sunup to sundown, and at night he was generally too tired to talk. He'd finish his supper, settle himself in his chair and doze off. Oh, it was an exciting life, all right! I read and I sewed and I darned and I cooked but after a while I began to get on my own nerves. Cathy, how I wished I had a baby!'

'With Dave dead,' Cathy pointed out, 'I think it's just as well that you didn't.'

'Y-es, I suppose so. Anyway, to go on, one day a friend of Dave's came out to the ranch. It seems this man had a chance to buy a good

45

ranch but he needed a partner who had some money to invest. Dave of course wasn't interested in it.'

'Was he the man who...?'

'Yes,' Gay said heavily. 'But I haven't come to that part of my story yet. His name was Chris. His last name is unimportant. There wasn't anything particularly attractive about him. He wasn't good looking, either. But he was warm and friendly and someone for me to talk to. He stayed with us over the week end, then he went back to town. Dave wasn't the same after Chris left. He told me very plainly that I had fallen in love with Chris.'

'How awful, Gay! What happened then?'

'O-h, we had a terrible quarrel. Dave lost his head and slapped me. I was more stunned than hurt. I got my things together and simply stalked out. Dave didn't try to stop me. I suppose he figured that after I'd cooled off, I'd come back. Besides, it was twenty miles to town and that's an awfully long way to go on foot.'

'I should think so!'

'Actually, Cathy, it wouldn't have mattered if it was fifty miles. I'd have gone regardless. I was suddenly free and that was all that mattered. I hadn't gotten very far when Chris rode up. He'd forgotten something at the house and he was going back for it. He could see that I'd been crying. I had to tell somebody what had happened, and I told

Chris. I suppose I shouldn't have, but I did. He gave me a lift into town. When we got there he took me to an elderly woman, a Mrs. Garvin who ran a small boarding house. She took me in. I got a job in the general store and managed to support myself after a fashion.'

'But what about Dave? When you didn't come back, did he do anything?'

'I heard nothing from Dave for a time, then one night when Chris was walking me home from the store, Dave rode into town.'

'Is that when it happened?'

'You mean the shooting? No. Dave ordered me to get my things and come back to the ranch. When I refused, he pushed me. Chris started for him but I stopped him. I told Dave I wasn't going back, at least not for a while. Dave got on his horse and rode away. But from that night on, he came to town regularly. I begged Chris not to come for me at the store, or at the house. Dave would follow me home, then he'd camp outside the house 'till Mrs. Garvin would bolt the front door and turn out the lights for the night, then he'd ride back to the ranch.'

'How long did that go on?'

'O-h, for about a week. Then Chris came to see me. What I was afraid of, happened. He'd fallen in love with me. He wanted me to go away with him. I told him that was ridiculous. The harder I tried to point out to him how perfectly impossible it was, the more dogged he became. Then he took to following me home, too. He and Dave had words and once I heard Dave tell him that it was the last warning he was going to give Chris to stay away from me. Then one night...'

'You needn't go on, Gay, if you don't want to.'

'I do want to. I want you to know everything that happened. Dave and Chris met just outside the store. Dave struck Chris, knocked him down, even went for his gun. I saw Chris lunge at Dave, saw them struggle with Chris trying to tear the gun out of Dave's hand. I heard a shot and Dave fell. I ran to him but he was dead when I reached his side.'

'And Chris? What happened to him?'

'He was dazed. He didn't realize what had happened. It was accidental and the Sheriff didn't hold him.'

Cathy threw back the covers, swung her legs over the side of the bed. She reached out, took Gay by the hand, brought Gay back to the bed with her, sat down beside her on the edge. Gay was sobbing now. Cathy put her arms around her sister, held her close.

'It's over now, Gay,' she said gently, comfortingly. 'It's been an awful experience, but you'll forget it in time. You simply mustn't think of it. And please, don't cry any more.'

She got to her feet.

'Come on,' she said authoritatively. 'You're going to get undressed and into bed. Sleep's the thing you need. In the morning you'll feel better for it. You'll see.'

Gay did not protest. Minutes later the two sisters lay beside each other. Gay's sobbing had ceased. She moved close to Cathy, burrowed under Cathy's comforting arm, settled herself and sighed.

'All right now?' Cathy asked.

'Oh, yes!' Gay answered.

'Then close your eyes,' Cathy commanded.

Gay obeyed. There was no further talk between them. Presently Gay's gentle breathing indicated that she was asleep. Cathy closed her eyes, but sleep did not come to her. She looked down at Gay, marveled at the ease with which she had fallen asleep. Cathy tossed and turned for an hour. Disturbing thoughts kept her awake. Always Phil Martin's face kept forcing its way into her thoughts. She was sure there was some significance attached to it and it worried her. Finally, she turned over on her side, closed her eyes fiercely and dozed off.

CHAPTER FOUR

THE LINE RIDER'S CABIN

The next few days passed swiftly though uneventfully. In the cottage, Nettie was herself again; Phil's planned reduction of food intake had been postponed a second time, and Nettie admitted quite freely that it was her fault. She felt that she owed Phil something ... accordingly another chocolate layer cake appeared on the supper table one evening and Phil's resolve disappeared in thin air. Of course he had needed but little encouragement, and aided and abetted by Nettie he managed without too much difficulty to reduce the cake to unimportant proportions. When Nettie asked him if he didn't want a little something before he went to bed, he rubbed his chin reflectively and considered it ... actually he was simply waiting, hopefully of course, for her to take things into her own hands. It was obvious that if she had a hand in it, he would feel better about it. Nettie smiled, placed the remains of the cake on the table before him, followed it with a fork, and finally with a glass of milk.

'Heck,' he said in surprise. 'Y'mean to say that's all that's left outta that whole cake?'

'That's all,' she replied.

'I'll be doggoned!'

'Go on,' she said. 'Eat it and let's go upstairs.'

That was all there was to that . . . and to the cake.

In the big house things ran along equally smoothly. In Cathy's capable hands, Gay's and George's wants were well attended to. Radiant as ever, Gay was the most carefree person on the ranch. As for Cathy, she was never without an apron. It seemed there was never an end to her work. It was late evening when George sauntered into the house, stopped and looked sharply at Cathy who was sitting at the kitchen table, a full sewing basket in her lap. He frowned, pushed his hat up from his eyes, hooked his thumbs in his belt, watched her for another minute. Finally she looked up.

'Don't you ever get 'ny time off?' he demanded.

'There's always something to do,' she answered with a patient smile. 'There are your socks.'

'Oh,' he said a bit lamely.

'I think you need a new pair of boots,' she went on gravely.

'S'matter with the ones I got?'

'We-ll,' she said, then she laughed and held up one sock and poked her clenched fist through a gap in the heel. 'See what I mean?'

He grinned boyishly.

'And how!' he said. 'I got another pair o' boots in my bag. I'll chuck these out pronto, the ones I'm wearin' now. And come t' think of it, ain't there a hull mess o' socks upstairs somewheres, that I ain't never even worn yet?'

'Yes. In your bureau.'

'Then f'r Pete's sake, chuck them doggoned things out!'

'All right,' she replied, rolled the torn sock and its mate into a ball, and put them aside. 'Your wish, m'lord, is my command.'

He grinned again. She eyed him for a moment.

'I wish you'd smile oftener,' she said. 'It does things for you.'

This time he made no comment.

'George,' she said and paused.

'Yeah?'

'I'm awf'lly glad you've changed your mind about leaving the Circle-A.'

'Who said I have?'

'No one,' she answered calmly. 'You're still here and I'm taking that to mean that you're staying. You ... you are staying, aren't you?'

'Not b'cause I want to!'

'Of course not.'

'There just ain't anything I c'n do about it,' he went on. 'Leastways, f'r the present anyway. There's that scrap I had with Corbin. I gotta stay around so he don't get

52

smart and take it out on somebody else.'

'I see.'

'Then there are them int'rest payments comin' up in a couple o' weeks. I can't walk out on them, c'n I?'

'No, you can't.'

'So there y'are. Somebody's gotta take care o' things, and fr'm what I c'n see of it, I'm the on'y one to do it.'

She nodded understandingly.

'Phil was telling me about the fences this morning.'

'What's the matter with them?'

'They need restringing.'

'O-h, yeah? We-ll, he's foreman, ain't he? Why don't he attend to th'm?'

'You're the owner,' she pointed out patiently. 'Why don't you ride out tomorrow and have a look at them for yourself?'

'I s'ppose I could do that all right,' he admitted.

'I think it would be a good idea.'

'I'll do it t'morrow. S-ay, you been outta the house t'day?'

'Today?' she repeated thoughtfully.

'Yeah ... t'day.'

'I ... I don't think so.'

'That's what I figgered. Put that stuff away.'

She looked at him questioningly.

'Go on,' he commanded. 'Get your coat and we'll go get us some air. It's a swell night out.'

She needed no further bidding. She caught up her basket, rose from her chair, flashed him a smile over her shoulder and went upstairs. He heard her quick step overhead ... when she returned, he was standing in the open doorway, staring out into the night. He straightened up, held the door for her, followed her out. It was a clear, cool night. There was a full, silvery moon in the limitless blue sky.

'Swell,' he said. 'Ain't it?'

'Beautiful,' she answered. 'Which way shall we go?'

He shrugged his shoulder.

'One way's the same as another t' me.'

They strolled past the house, turned in the direction of the corral. There was a handful of men idling in front of the bunkhouse. They heard the plunking of a banjo, then a man's voice was raised in song. Mechanically both Cathy and George stopped. The song came drifting toward them.

'I don't think I've ever heard that before,' Cathy said.

He grinned again ... in the moonlight his even teeth gleamed white and bright.

'Name of it's Harriet,' he said.

'Oh!'

'Ain't surprised you never heard it b'fore,' he went on. 'Somebody down in Texas made it up.'

'Is that where you learned it?'

'Nope. A girl taught it t' me. Boy, and could she sing it!'

'They're singing it again,' she said.

Harr-iet, oh, Harr-iet . . .
All the cowboys want to marry Harriet
'Cause Harriet's so handy with a lariat;
But Harriet doesn't want to marry yet
    'Cause she's havin' too much fun.

'You shoulda heard Pat sing it,' George said. 'That was somethin' worth hearin'.'

'Her name was . . . Pat?'

'Yeah, short f'r Patricia. And she was just about the prettiest girl I ever saw.'

'You liked her a lot, didn't you?'

'I sure did. Bet she don't know what t' make o' me not hustlin' back like I said I'd do,' he mused.

'Was she . . . is she . . . young?'

'Heck, yes,' he said quickly. 'Don't imagine she's a day more'n eighteen, if she's even that old.'

She was silent now, and motionless, too, with her chin buried in the folds of her buttoned-up coat collar and her hands jammed deep down in her pockets.

'You'd like 'er. Don't know anybody who don't.'

'Do you know her very long?'

'O-h, sure! Know 'er ever since she was, we-ll, since she was about eight, I'd say. She's Joe Carson's sister.'

'Joe ... Carson?'

'Uh-huh. He owns the show, y'know.'

'I see.'

'Y'know, I've up and quit the show more'n a dozen times, every doggoned time Joe and me had words. If it wasn't f'r Pat, b'lieve me, Joe woulda never seen me again after the first time I quit.'

'You mean you stayed on because of her?'

'She allus talked me outta quittin'.'

'Does she perform, too?'

'Pat?' He laughed. 'After livin' most of 'er life with a rodeo, you'd think she could do most anything with a horse. Fact o' the matter is, Pat's just about the worst rider I ever saw. But even though she don't do 'nything in the show, she's just as much a part uv it as if she did.'

She pawed the ground with the toe of her shoe. He watched her for a moment ... when she stopped, he looked at her questioningly.

'S'matter?' he asked. 'Cold?'

'Y-es,' she said a bit hesitantly. 'Besides, it's getting late and I think I'd better go inside. You don't mind, do you?'

'Nope,' he answered and his casualness made her bristle. 'Y'know, Pat allus used t' c'mplain about the cold. Reckon most girls do, too, don't they?'

'I'm afraid I wouldn't know about most girls,' she said sharply and promptly regretted the tone she had used. In an effort to make

56

amends she added quickly: 'But you needn't go in yet.'

He hitched up his belt.

'I'll walk back to the house with you,' he said briefly.

They turned, walked back in silence. When they reached the kitchen door, he stepped ahead of her, opened it, held it wide for her.

'Good night,' she said over her shoulder.

'G'night,' he answered.

She was midway between the door and the stairway when the door slammed. She frowned with annoyance, quickened her pace. Gay was in bed, reading, propped up with both of their pillows behind her back when Cathy entered their room. Gay looked up, smiled knowingly, closed her book and put it down on the chair beside her.

'Back rather soon,' she said. 'Aren't you?'

Cathy did not answer. She unbuttoned her coat, whipped it off, threw it into the arm chair at the window. Gay's eyebrows arched.

'Oh!' she said significantly. 'So that's how it is!'

Cathy whirled around.

'I could shake him!' she said angrily.

'He's a bit too big for that, don't you think? I'm afraid you'll have to punish him some other way.'

'He can be the most aggravating man when he wants to,' Cathy said loudly.

'And this was one of those times, I take it.'

'All he talked of was a girl.'

Gay's eyebrows arched again.

'Indeed!'

'Her name is Pat,' Cathy went on. She unbuttoned her dress, stopped, turned for a moment to make certain that the door was locked, then she finished the unbuttoning and slipped the dress off. 'She's eighteen, she's divine, and quite the most beautiful thing he's ever seen.'

'That's the first time I ever heard of a man using that approach,' Gay commented.

'She sings like a thrush, and if it wasn't for her, he'd have quit the rodeo he's been with long ago. She talked him out of quitting.'

'How touching!'

'She has one weakness. Horses.'

'You mean she can't get enough of them?'

'Oh, no!' Cathy said quickly. 'She's helpless when a horse enters the picture. It seems that despite the fact that she's lived with horses most of her beautiful young life, she's never really learned how to ride them. That's the story of Patricia Carson. That was all Mister Akers could talk about. Interesting, don't you think?'

'Not particularly,' Gay answered. She paused for a moment, then: 'Cathy.'

'Yes?'

'I've probably never noticed it before, but were your eyes always so green?'

'If you mean that I'm jealous, you're

wrong,' Cathy said indignantly. She yanked on her nightgown, smoothed it down. 'I'm not the slightest bit interested in Mister Akers, and that goes double for the women in his life. So there!'

Gay returned Cathy's pillow to its proper place, adjusted her own.

'Come on, angel,' she said. 'Sleep's the thing you need. In the morning you'll feel better for it. I think that's quoting you pretty accurately, isn't it?'

Cathy did not reply. She turned out the lamp light, climbed into bed. They lay in silence for a time.

'Gay.'

'Yes?'

'You lived in Texas. Did you ever hear anyone sing "Harriet"?'

'Oh, yes! I think it's rather cute.'

• 'I think it's silly!' Cathy retorted. She pulled up the covers with a vengeance. 'The very beautiful Patricia sang "Harriet" so divinely, it left Mister Akers enraptured. He's never gotten over it, and the chances are, he never will. I know I'll never like that song because any time I hear it, it will always remind me of dear, dear Patricia, and heaven knows, I don't ever want to be reminded of her!'

Gay turned her back to Cathy, stifled her laugh by burying her face in her pillow.

'I'm glad you find it so amusing,' Cathy

said stiffly. She turned on her side. 'GOOD NIGHT!'

★   ★   ★

It was about three o'clock the next afternoon when Gay, booted and clad in a sweater and dungarees, emerged from the house. Cathy followed her to the door, eyed her critically.

'Going riding?' Cathy asked. 'Thought you'd had enough of horses the other day?'

'That was the other day,' Gay answered lightly.

'We-ll...'

'Besides,' Gay added. 'You don't want me to be like Patricia, do you?'

Cathy closed the door without another word. Gay laughed softly, strolled around the house and sauntered off in the direction of the corral. She had almost reached it when a horseman came whirling out ... it was George Akers. He looked up, spied her, jerked his mount to a stop. He eased himself in the saddle, ran his eye over her.

'You aimin' to do some ridin'?' he asked.

'I had planned to,' she replied calmly. 'You don't mind, do you?'

'N-o, reckon not,' he said with equal calm. 'After all, it's your neck you're riskin' so it's awright with me.'

Gay smiled up at him ... inwardly she was experiencing Cathy's desire to shake him.

'Thank you,' she said sweetly. 'I was afraid you might have some fears about the horse's neck.'

He frowned, spurred his mount and dashed away. Gay's eyes followed him for a moment, then she strode briskly to the corral gate, opened it, and stepped into the enclosure. There were a dozen horses idling close by . . . they turned and trotted off. A single horse . . . Gay noted that he was fully saddled . . . detached himself from the others and jogged forward. He stopped in front of her, nudged her. Gay patted the animal's neck. She looked about her quickly . . . there was no one else in sight; she caught up the reins, gripped the saddle horn and swung herself up astride the horse, wheeled him and rode out. She heard a voice yell, 'hey, hold on there!' frowned and muttered, 'damn,' and reluctantly pulled up. She twisted around in the saddle . . . a man came running toward her from the direction of the bunkhouse.

'Where'n hell d'you think you're going with that horse, huh?' he sputtered breathlessly. He panted to a stop in front of her, looked up, reddened and swallowed. 'O-h, excuse me, Ma'm. Didn't know it was you. Reckon them pants o' yourn fooled me.'

Gay smiled down at him.

'Is he yours?' she asked, patting the horse's neck.

The puncher grinned.

'Yep,' he replied. 'All uv 'er.'

'Oh!' Gay said and laughed. 'Were you going to ride her?'

'I was,' the man answered. 'But what I was gonna do ain't so important that I can't put it off f'r t'morrow. Fact o' the matter is, Ma'm, I'm even glad to have 'n excuse f'r not doin' it t'day.'

'We-ll . . .'

'You go right ahead, Ma'm,' he continued. 'When you bring 'er back, all you hafta do is turn 'er loose in the corral. She'll be awright there 'till I get around to tendin' to 'er.'

'Thank you.'

Gay wheeled the mare.

'Oh, Ma'm!'

Gay reined in again, looked back over her shoulder.

'Her name's Molly,' the puncher added. 'She handles plumb easy and you don't hafta be afraid o' her none.'

Gay nodded and jogged away. The puncher watched them for a moment, then he hitched up his belt, turned and trudged off toward the bunkhouse. Gay circled the corral . . . some of the horses in the enclosure poked their noses through the bars, eyed them and whinnied. The mare answered with a snort and a toss of her head, and clattered away. They neared the barn. Gay looked over . . . there were two men in front of the building working over a broken wagon wheel; the men looked up, when the mare came abreast of the barn, they touched their hats gravely. Gay acknowledged with a smile. Presently they were in the open. Gay settled herself in the saddle, tightened her grip on the reins, nudged Molly with her knees. The mare responded, broke into an easy-gained canter. They went downhill and the ranch dropped away behind them.

There was no sign of George and Gay frowned when she thought of him. She wondered where he had gone, found herself scanning the range for sight of him. She flicked the loose ends of the reins lightly over Molly's neck and the mare lengthened her stride. A mile slipped away, then another, and finally a third and a fourth. From then on time and distance lost their meaning. It was quite a bit later when Gay spied a distant gust of dust spiraling into the sky.

'There's George now,' she heard herself say. 'That's the dust from his horse's hoofs.'

She experienced an inward glow of satisfaction at having overtaken him. The smile that appeared and hovered for a brief moment at the corners of her mouth reflected her satisfaction.

'I'd like to teach him a lesson,' she said but inwardly again there wasn't any such thought or desire.

She wondered why she had said it since she hadn't meant it. All her life she had said one thing when she had meant another. Sometimes it puzzled her, even worried her, but not for very long. She had always found it difficult to explain some of the things she did ... she was impetuous, admittedly, and when she got into difficulties she was always surprised, even hurt, when no one else saw things the way she did.

There was that time when she went riding with Will Herber. She was sixteen and he was eighteen. Will was tall and strong and good looking and every girl in the county was wild about him. A sudden rainstorm overtook them about ten miles from home and forced them to take shelter in an old abandoned barn. The roof was leaky and they huddled together in a dark corner with Will's protective arm around her. The steady thump of the rain on the roof and the walls lulled her to sleep. She awoke when Will kissed her ... only she kept her eyes closed to let him think she was still asleep. He kissed her again and again, but she made no attempt to stop him. He was a 'nice' boy, clean and wholesome-looking, and he enjoyed kissing her, why should she stop him? She was warm and comfortable in his strong young arms, and his kisses were neither thrilling nor objectionable. It was like being served something you'd never eaten before ... you tasted it, swallowed it, satisfied your host and that was all there was to it.

Of course, when Will's trembling and clammy hands began to stray, she 'awoke,' simply pushed his hands away, and got to her feet. Instead of putting on a great show of maidenly and virtuous indignation, followed by an outburst of tears and climaxed by slapping his face, she smoothed down her dress, tucked in a couple of stray strands of hair, and walked out of the barn. Will, red-faced and completely miserable, followed at her heels. He helped her mount to the single seat in the currey, climbed up beside her. They drove home in silence, with Will afraid to even glance in her direction. When they pulled up in front of her house, Will helped her down, then he fairly leaped up again on the seat, whipped up his horse and drove away at top speed.

Gay's mother proved to be more of a problem than Will had been. She was aghast when Gay told her about the currey ride and the barn episode. She scolded Gay for having encouraged the youth, accused her of having invited trouble, and foresaw a terrible end for her. Gay was considerably taken back ... she couldn't understand why her mother ranted so since nothing had happened to her. As a result, she never confided in her again. That night, with her bedroom door locked to prevent intrusion, she stood nude before her mirror and studied her reflection. She had never done that before. She was agreeably surprised, in fact, she was quite pleased with what she saw.

Then there was the affair with Chris. She had never blamed herself for what had happened. She had refused to accept any responsibility for it. She hadn't encouraged Chris' attentions to her ... he had been attracted to her. She admitted she liked men ... men always eyed her with admiration, while women looked at her enviously. Was she to blame for the undeniable fact that she was pretty and attractive? If a man lost his head over a pretty woman, was it the woman's fault? Of course not!

There was but one thing she hadn't told Cathy in her hysterical and tearful recital of her life as Dave Hollis' wife ... it was something she refused to let herself recall. She simply dropped a curtain over the incident and put it out of her mind.

Chris had taken her to the boarding house only to find the place darkened and locked up. The hotel was out of the question ... there were a dozen townsmen idling in front of the place and for the first time in her life Gay shied away from admiring eyes and glances. She was too tired. Chris' place was close by, and he took her there. They talked far into the night, and then when her eyes began to close, he insisted that she stay there for the night. Hastily he assured her that she would be all right ... there was a lock on the bedroom door. She hesitated at first, finally accepted. Chris rolled himself up in a blanket and stretched out on a couple of chairs. He awoke when he heard her sobbing. He tiptoed to the bedroom door and listened there for a moment. He shook his head sadly . . . she was crying, he told himself, because of Dave. He had no way of knowing that Gay was sobbing because she was sympathizing with herself, and tears offered her the only way of expressing her self-sympathy. Her sobbing continued and he rapped on the door . . . when she did not answer his repeated knocking, he touched the door knob, turned it and opened the door. Gay had forgotten to lock it.

He knelt down beside her, tried to comfort her . . . she was like a child, she whimpered, sat up, sobbed against his chest, and finally quieted down. When he tried to lay her down, she clung to him, drew him down, too. She nestled in his arms, dozed off . . . he tried to get up but she refused to let him go. As the night wore on, it grew colder. Chris lifted the end of her blanket, draped it over his body and shoulder . . . he dozed off presently. Their first sleep was short-lived, but because of the darkness neither knew when the other awoke. She knew he was awake when she felt his hands on her. She did not move. Later both of them fell into a deep sleep, but curiously it was of Will Herber that Gay dreamed.

They awoke at dawn. Each was flushed and uneasy. Neither dared look at the other. Chris dressed quickly and left the place ... Gay had no alternative but to stay. At ten o'clock Chris returned. Mrs. Garvin had returned some time during the night. He handed Gay some money ... she had none of her own and accepted Chris' without question or thought. He suggested that she go at once to Mrs. Garvin's place. Later that day, after she had been installed in the boarding house, he appeared there, told her of a job she could obtain.

Her thoughts went back to George Akers. He hadn't made much of a fuss over her ... that was a new experience for her; ever since she could remember, everyone had made a great 'to do' about her, especially the men. With the years she had come to expect their attentions and admiration as something due her. She knew she was pretty ... hadn't she always been told that?

Gay suddenly awoke to the realization that the mare had halted. She flicked the reins again and the startled Molly dashed off again. But fifteen minutes hard riding availed them nothing ... The spiraling dust had disappeared and George was still unfound. She glanced skyward ... there was a gathering of dark clouds directly above her. For a minute she debated with herself to turn back or go on. Stubbornly she decided to go on. The sky grew darker and the mare whinnied and slackened her pace ... when Gay did not urge her on, she stopped altogether.

Gay stood up in the stirrups. She scanned the range again. Southward, probably a mile away, was a small building. She wondered if George had gone there. She dropped down into the saddle, gripped the reins anew.

'Go on,' she said and jerked the reins.

Molly cantered off. There was a sudden clap of thunder ... it rolled over the equally suddenly blackened range with the frightening and breathtaking crash of massed cannon fire. The mare stiffened ... a second peal of thunder made her scream with terror. She bolted away so suddenly that Gay was nearly thrown. She dropped the reins, never to regain them ... frantically she threw herself forward, clutched at the saddle horn and gripped it grimly with both hands. Now the rain burst upon them. It pelted them unmercifully, with huge raindrops that seemed and sounded like drumming hailstones. Gay bowed her head. In the blackness that obscured everything, the plunging mare tripped over a half-buried rock, fell to her knees, and Gay was hurled over Molly's head. Miraculously, she landed on her hands and knees and sprawled out on her face, breathless and stunned.

Molly struggled to her feet whimpering. She hobbled over to Gay's side, whinnied, nudged her pleadingly. There was no response from the prostrate Gay. The mare turned away reluctantly, looked back once or twice, then she limped away into the enveloping darkness. Probably ten minutes later Gay stirred. She opened her eyes ... she sobbed brokenly, hysterically, climbed to her feet, panting for breath. She turned quickly, looked about her frantically.

'Molly!' she gasped. 'Molly!'

There was no answering whinny, no hoof beat to reassure her that she was not alone ... there was nothing but the drenching downpour and the swirling rain-laden wind that lashed her and stung her. She stumbled away blindly. The wind whipped her wet hair wildly. She tripped and fell, scrambled to her feet, stumbled and fell again ... she got up and forced herself on. She walked and ran and plodded ahead, half blinded by the rain and the wind. How she ever managed to reach the cabin, she never knew. She fell against the door, it yielded when she turned the knob and she fell inside. She struggled to her knees, twisted around and managed to slam the door shut. She sobbed again weakly and brokenly, sagged and suddenly toppled over in a limp heap.

CHAPTER FIVE

PARTNERS OF THE STORM

Phil Martin huddled within his rain-soaked jacket and its soggy upturned collar. His hat brim was shapeless beneath the downpour, his pants were drenched and his boots were waterlogged. His equally rain-soaked horse plodded along wearily ... he was too worn and winded to go any faster and Phil was too much annoyed with things in general to care.

'Damn the luck,' he muttered for the hundredth time. 'Damn the luck anyway. If I'da got goin' an hour sooner, I'da missed this. The worst that coulda happened woulda been that I'da been close enough t' home t' hafta ride f'r it like hell, but after that I'da been home 'stead of out here. Now it's so blamed dark, I'm doggoned if I know where we're goin'. F'r all I know, we might even be headed away fr'm home 'stead o' goin' toward it. Damn the luck!'

He reached up, took off his hat and beat it against his leg. Rain pelted him and the wind whipped his hair about wildly. He clapped his hat on again, pulled the brim down, settled himself in the saddle.

'I c'n picture Nettie,' he muttered again. 'Bet she's just about fit t' be tied. She's

71

probably been pacin' the floor and squattin' at the window, staring out into space, and by now she's probably talkin' to 'erself. "That big fool," she's sayin'. "Everyone else is home where everyone belongs. But not my husband. He doesn't know enough to come in outta the rain." Sure, I'm a dummy. I like bein' out here. I like gettin' so danged soaked.'

He sneezed suddenly and his head was jerked up. He sniffled, drew his wet sleeve across his mouth.

'It's awright f'r her t' bellyache,' he went on. 'Oh, sure. She don't hafta ride fences and fix 'em. I do. Still, she does all the bellyachin' anyway. "You're foreman," she said this mornin'. "Why must you do that work? Why can't one of the others do it?" It's allus why this and why that. She keeps yammerin' and yammerin', and you'd think she'd get so doggoned sick an' tired o' hearin' 'er own voice, she'd shut up. But o-h, no! Not Nettie. She goes on and on. Sometimes I wonder if she don't hafta stop an' take a breath.'

Then wind tore at his hat, strove mightily to rip it off his head . . . he used both hands to pull it down more securely.

'B'lieve me,' he mumbled. 'It's a damn good thing I got outta the house when I did this mornin'. If I hadn'ta, we'da sure had it out hot an' heavy. Feller c'n stand just so much. After that he gotta do somethin' or

72

bust.'

His horse stumbled and Phil jerked him to his feet.

'Don't you go actin' up now,' Phil warned him. 'Then there's somethin' else. Since that mornin' when I stopped Gay's horse when he was hightailin' it away hell bent f'r election, Nettie ain't been the same. O-h, I know there are times when she seems t' be, but most o' the time she ain't. I ketch 'er watchin' me sometimes, queer-like. You'd think it was my fault that Gay kissed me. Doggone it, anyway!'

He rode on for a time in silence, a bulky figure with a bowed head. His weary horse stopped suddenly, and Phil's head jerked upward. Fifty feet ahead of them was a dark structure.

'What in time...' Phil muttered. He jerked the reins sharply. 'Go on!'

The horse broke into a trot ... Phil lashed him with the loose ends of the reins. Presently they pulled up in front of the building and Phil dismounted stiffly. He trudged to the door. He turned the knob. The door opened a bit and he looked surprised. He pushed it, and it opened wider ... he put his shoulder to it and the door opened even wider.

'H'm,' he muttered. 'What d'you know!'

He poked his head inside, but it was too dark for him to see anything. He stepped into the shack, stopped when he stumbled over something that lay on the floor. He drew back warily, whipped open his jacket, loosened his gun in its holster ... he dug into an inside pocket, produced a match. The phosphorous head scratched against his thumb nail and flared. Phil's eyes ranged downward and widened almost instantly ... on the floor lay the huddled figure of a girl.

'Holy cow!' he whispered in awed tones.

He stepped a bit closer and bent over. It was Gay Hollis. The match seared his fingers and he dropped the curling ember hastily, soothed his fingers with his tongue, then he quickly dug into his pocket again for more matches. Another flamed shortly. There was a shadeless lamp standing on a shelf directly opposite the door; he strode over, tried the wick, touched the match flame to it and it flamed with a sputtering light. Phil closed the door quickly. He whipped off his hat and jacket, slung them aside, placed the lamp on the floor just beyond the exhausted Gay. He knelt down beside her.

'Hey,' he said, touched her arm. 'Hey!'

There was no response from the girl. He turned her over gently on her back. She was breathing and he felt relieved. He raised his eyes. There was a wide bunk at the far end of the shack and a folded blanket lay at the foot of the bunk itself. He slid his left arm under her, his right arm under her legs ... he lifted her easily, carried her to the bunk and started to lay her down. He frowned in thought for a moment, finally shook his head.

'Nope,' he muttered. 'Cain't put 'er down the way she is. Gotta get them wet things o' hers off first.'

He swung her around, sat her down on the edge of the bunk, sat down beside her with his left arm around her ... she sagged against his shoulder. He twisted around, grunted, began to pull up her sweater ... he stopped, frowned again. He backed away from her a bit, held her upright with his left hand and unbuttoned her dungarees. Something pink peered out at him and he stopped hastily ... he rubbed his chin with his big right thumb. Presently he straightened up and laid her down. He caught up the blanket, opened it and spread it over her. Then he knelt down, fumbled underneath the blanket and managed to complete the unbuttoning of her dungarees. He slipped his left hand under her body, used it as a lever and raised her ... presently he slipped off the dungarees, pulled them out from under the blanket and straightened up again. He looked around the place. There were a couple of upended boxes beyond the door ... he strode over, draped the wet dungarees over one box and retraced his steps. Again he bent over her, remembered that she was still wearing her boots ... after some more fumbling under the blanket he removed them, put them down on the floor. He eyed her sweater again. That was going to prove even more difficult than the dungarees.

His left arm helped prop her up ... after some clumsy efforts he managed to get her right arm out of the sweater sleeve, then he turned her a bit, and freed her left arm.

'Doggone,' he muttered and shook his head.

He squared his shoulders, drew a deep breath ... he drew up her sweater, gulped and colored. Quickly he eased it over her head, backed away and came erect. He turned, marched off, and draped the sweater over a second box.

'Boy,' he mumbled and shook his head again. 'That was somethin', awright. Danged good thing Nettie wasn't here t' see it.'

He trudged back, stood beside the bunk and looked down at her, watched her for a moment. He heard a whinny outside, wheeled and went striding out. The rain was still beating down. He circled the shack looking for something that might provide some sort of cover for his horse. He tripped over something ... it was a folded-up tarpaulin and he opened it quickly. He slung one end of the tarpaulin up on the edge of the shack's roof ... he picked up a rock, used it to weight down the canvas end; he scouted around as best he could, found half a dozen more rocks and presently the improvised shelter was completed. He backed his horse into it, turned and dashed back inside. His shirt was drenched and it clung to him. He found a battered pail in a dark corner of the shack, brought it out ... with his gun butt he smashed the two remaining boxes, put the pieces of wood into the pail, used two of his precious remaining matches to start the wood burning. When the pail fire appeared to be coming along, he put the thing down in the middle of the floor, moved it a little closer to the boxes holding Gay's sweater and dungarees.

'Reckon that oughta help th'm dry,' he muttered.

He unbuttoned his own shirt, took it off ... held it up for a moment; there was a makeshift table in one corner and he dragged it across the floor until it was close to the cracking pail, spread his shirt out on the table with the tail hanging down. He felt of his pants leg.

'Wish I could take 'em off too,' he said.

In the corner in which the table had stood was a small chest. He strode over to it, raised the lid ... he bent down, fumbled in its dark insides, straightened up shortly. In his arms was another blanket. He opened it, whipped it around him, pulled off his wet boots, then he took off his pants. He moved his shirt a bit in order to make room on the table for the pants. When he was finished, he stood looking down into the fire in the pail; he turned slowly, sauntered across the floor in his stocking feet to where Gay lay. The lamp light flickered and went out.

'Damn,' he said aloud.

'Phil,' he heard a voice say and a hand reached out and caught his.

'O-h,' he said. 'You awright?'

'Yes,' Gay answered. 'Thanks to you of course.'

'Heck,' he said. 'Wasn't anything much I did.'

'Perhaps,' she said. 'Still I think I owe you my life twice.'

He laughed ... it was a hollow laugh, intended to help him cover up his embarrassment at her praise.

'You're sweet,' she went on. 'And I like you.'

He managed a better sounding laugh this time.

'G'wan,' he retorted. 'That ain't what my wife says about me.'

He moved away a bit, held the blanket tighter around him. Her hand caught one end of it.

'Don't go,' she pleaded. 'Sit down here beside me.'

'We-ll ...' He sat down on the edge of the bunk. 'There. That awright?'

There was a movement on the bunk and

Gay pushed the outspread blanket away and sat up.

'Hey,' he said quickly. 'I don't think you oughta do that.'

'Do what, Phil? This?' Her lips were against his, her arm around his neck, before he realized it. 'Don't you want me to thank you?'

She kissed him softly, gently. Phil was mute ... he knew he should have said something, perhaps done something, but he was incapable of either. Her arm came down again, but she did not move away. There was no explaining what followed. Perhaps it was the darkness that was responsible for what followed. Whatever it was, Phil surrendered to its whispered urgings, willingly, even eagerly. He caught Gay in his arms, crushed her to him, kissed her loudly and hungrily, kissed her as he had never kissed Nettie. Gay did not resist him. His lips covered her face, her lips, her cheeks and her eyes, then downward to her throat.

'Phil!' she whispered when he raised his head. 'Phil!'

He kissed her again and again. She ran her fingers through his wet hair, then she sank down and drew him down with her.

George Akers took refuge from the storm in another line rider's shack some miles farther east. He burst into the place with a sigh of relief after stabling his horse in the sturdy lean-to behind the shack. He took off his wet jacket, slung it over the table that stood against the wall, hunted around by match light for a lamp. He passed the single window and the wind and rain that poured through brought him to a surprised and abrupt stop. He found upon examination that there was no window pane in the window frame.

'O-h, fine,' he muttered.

He retraced his steps to the table, caught up his jacket and carried it to the window, hung it over the glassless frame.

'Reckon that oughta do it,' he said and turned away.

The wind whipped it off the window and sent it whirling back at him. He slammed it down on the table. There was a bunk directly below the level of the window ... it was wet and dirty.

'Now why'n hell would anybody put a bunk right smack under a window?' he muttered. 'Might as well've put it up on the roof.'

Match light revealed a folded blanket at the foot of the bunk ... George picked it up and spread it out. It was just as wet as the bunk and even dirtier. His lips curled in mingled scorn and disgust and he cast it back. He probed the rest of the shack but there was neither lamp nor food. The one discovery that surprised him consisted of a chair that still

80

retained its back rest and its four legs. He dragged it away to a far corner, slammed it against the wall and finally seated himself.

'This is what I call somethin' awright,' he muttered. 'A bunk that needs a delousin', a blanket that oughta be burned up, a window without a pane o' glass, one chair, no lamp an' no grub. Doggone it, the first thing I'm gonna do when I get back is have Phil load up a wagon with stuff an' run it out here. An' he's gonna hafta fix that danged window, too.'

He leaned back in the chair.

'Why'n hell I came out here so late in the afternoon is somethin' I'll never understand,' he mumbled. 'I oughta go have m' head examined. Mebbe there's somethin' wrong with me and I don't know it.'

He got up, tilted the chair back against the wall, seated himself again, hooked his booted heels in the chair's lower rung. He whipped up his shirt collar, buttoned it around his neck, pulled down his hat brim, dug his hands deep into his pants pockets. He was tired and presently his eyes closed. He opened them once or twice, raised his head, too, listened to the steady downbeat of the rain . . . he shook his head each time, settled himself in the chair, and finally, he dozed off.

He awoke with a start, looked about him quickly. He got to his feet, winced and made a wry face . . . his neck was stiff as were his arms and legs. He rubbed his neck for a moment, stamped up and down, rubbed his arms. He trudged to the window and peered out. The night had gone and in its stead the sky was filled with a drab light. It was nearly dawn. The rain too had ceased and now the air was heavy with the smell of wet earth and soggy damp clothes.

'That's that,' he said. He caught up his jacket, slung it over his shoulder. 'I'm gonna make tracks f'r home, get me a lotta hot grub, then I'm gonna hit the hay and sleep f'r a week.'

He stalked out of the shack, swung around it to the lean-to at the rear. He pushed the door open and plodded inside. His horse neighed a greeting. George eyed him, touched the walls, looked down at the straw and hay on the ground. The animal neighed a second time.

'Awright,' George said gruffly. 'Quit crowin'. So you were warm an' comfortable in here while I half froze t' death in there. Awright, awright. If I'da had 'ny sense we'da swapped places and that woulda been that. But I let you stay put so shut up.'

George saddled up, led the horse outside. He slung his wet jacket over the saddle horn, swung himself up, dug his booted feet into the stirrups, reached for the reins.

'Go on,' he commanded.

The horse jogged away. The wet ground

muffled his hoof beats. The mist had lifted now and the strong smell of wet earth had lessened. They rode for a time in silence . . . it grew a bit warmer as the light in the sky deepened. George paid little attention to it . . . his thoughts were elsewhere.

'Boy,' he muttered. 'What I wouldn't give f'r a stack o' hot cakes and some coffee! Bet Cathy's makin' 'em this mornin', leastways when she gets up. I c'n almost smell 'em way out here and what they're doin' t' me is nobody's business. Doggone it, once I get back there, I'm damned if I do a single thing but eat and sleep, then I'm gonna eat s'me more and sleep s'me more. Feller's plumb loco t' do anything else if he don't hafta.'

The horse turned his head and looked up at him.

'Yeah?' George demanded. 'What d'you want? I ain't talkin' t' you anyway, so s'ppose you mind your own business and stick t' your job o' gettin' me home. You heard me, so get goin'!'

The thought of Cathy's hot cakes left him thinking about Cathy herself.

'There's a funny kid,' he mused. 'Sometimes I don't get her nowhow. Seems I never know how t' take 'er. Lookit the way she suddenly froze up on me when I was gassin' about Pat. O-h, I suppose I was layin' it on kind o' thick about Pat, but she shouldn'ta taken on like she did. Heck, what's Pat t' me? On'y the boss' sister. And a feller's gotta be nice to the boss' sister, ain't he? Cathy shoulda been able t' figger that much out f'r 'erself. 'Stead she froze up and went in. Aw, girls give me a pain, doggone 'em!'

George was silent for the next half mile.

'That Cathy ain't a bad lookin' kid,' he began again. 'Course she ain't a looker like 'er sister, Gay, but that baby is somethin' I don't want too much of. I'm kinda leery o' her. I wish t' hell she'd quit wearin' dungarees and as f'r them shirts, we-ll mebbe they're awright f'r men. They ain't f'r her. An' what gets me is the way she wears th'm. She don't use half the buttons. Noticed the way the boys look at her. She don't leave much t' their imagination. If she was my sister, I'd sure warm 'er fanny. Mebbe that's what she's never had and needs.'

His horse had made no effort to quicken his pace and George eyed him and frowned.

'S'matter with you?' he demanded finally. 'Where d'you think we're goin' ... to a picnic? Come on, shake yourself, an' get movin'. I'm wet and I'm hungry and I wanna get home. So get goin' b'fore I start wallopin' that fanny o' yourn. Get goin', y'hear?'

The animal evidently heard and understood for he lengthened his stride without further delay.

'That's better,' George grunted and settled

himself in the saddle.

Suddenly the horse jerked his head up and whinnied. George sat up again.

'Huh?' he asked. 'S'matter now?'

There was a shack directly ahead of them and George looked it over carefully.

'Wonder how I come t' miss that last night?' he asked himself. He nudged the horse with his knees. 'Go 'head.'

They rode up to the shack, halted a dozen feet from it. George spotted the makeshift tarpaulin shelter that Phil had rigged up. Phil's horse poked his head out of the canvas folds, then he emerged, plodded forward to meet them. George's eyes ranged over the animal ... there was a Circle-A brand on his hip. George dismounted, trudged around the shack to the front, jerked the door knob.

'Hey,' he called, then he turned the knob and the door opened. He pushed it open wider, stepped over the threshold. There was a stirring in the bunk at the far end of the shack, and he turned and looked in its direction. His lips tightened. 'Oh,' he said aloud, turned and tramped out.

He pulled the door shut behind him, started off toward his horse, slackened his pace and finally stopped altogether.

'Well!' he said. 'What d'you know 'bout that!'

He fumbled in his pants pocket, produced a damp and crumpled package of tobacco, rolled himself a cigarette, lighted it and inhaled deeply. He heard the shack door open again and he looked back over his shoulder. Phil Martin trudged out, stopped and retraced his steps and pulled the door shut.

'Better tell 'er t' get 'er things on,' George called curtly.

Phil's face was flushed and streaky.

'She ... she's doin' that,' he answered. 'She won't be more'n a minute.'

George flipped his cigarette away. He swung himself up into the saddle. Martin came striding up to him. Their eyes met briefly.

'Look, George,' Phil began.

'Yeah?'

'There's a heap more t' this than you think,' Phil said. 'I don't mean that none uv it's my fault and that it's all hers. It ain't.'

There was no reply. Phil hitched up his pants, drew a deep breath.

'You aimin' to tell Nettie about this?' he asked.

'Nope,' George said evenly. 'That's your business.'

Phil looked relieved.

'You can tell 'er anything you like,' George concluded. 'She's your wife, y'know, not mine.'

'Sure,' Phil said, nodding. 'And thanks.'

Gay came out of the shack. Phil stepped forward, grabbed his horse's bridle, swung him around. Gay marched up to them . . . she looked up at George but he turned his head, then he wheeled his horse away.

'We'd better get goin',' he said over his shoulder. 'B'fore they come lookin' f'r us.'

Phil helped Gay mount his horse, then he climbed up behind her. Presently they came loping up, ranged themselves alongside George's horse. They rode for a time in silence, each of them grave-faced and thoughtful.

'Phil,' George said. 'You'd better tell th'm that the three uv us spent the night in the shack. There ain't 'ny point in hurtin' Nettie anymore'n you have already.'

CHAPTER SIX

AFTERMATH

It was three days since the storm, three long, drawnout and uneventful days. To all appearances there was nothing amiss in either the cottage or the big house, yet the evidence of strained relationships was there. It hung like a pall over both households; one sensed it in the immediate atmosphere, read it in the tightened faces of those concerned, noticed it in their relationship with one another.

As one would expect, it was even more

noticeable in the cottage. Perhaps it was due to Phil whose guilty conscience goaded him into doing the very things that were certain to arouse doubts and suspicions in his wife. Admittedly, Nettie was a jealous woman ... hence, given cause, it was only natural that she should begin to wonder about her husband. She had a fertile and extremely inflammatory imagination, and given a lead upon which to build and enlarge, her imagination knew no bounds. In her mind's eye she had stored away the scene she had witnessed of Gay kissing Phil as a 'reward' for saving her life the day her horse bolted with her. As time went on that picture became a bit dimmed ... now she resurrected it, dusted it off, brought it out into the light. It was equally natural then that Nettie's conjecturing should lead her to connect Gay with Phil's curious behaviour. But Nettie had learned something since that episode ... never again, she had promised herself, would Phil know that she was jealous.

There was no telling now, no knowing just what Nettie thought of and believed of Phil's awkwardly told story of how he and George had been overtaken by the storm, of how they had headed for the only available shelter, the line rider's shack, of how they had stumbled over Gay whose horse had thrown her and left her to find her stumbling way in the swirling storm as best she could, of how they had managed to get her to safety, too, and finally, how the three of them had spent the night together in the limited confines of the shack.

Nettie had listened to Phil's recital, but she had offered no comment when he had finished. Her silence had made him uncomfortable and he began to sense that Nettie, with her usual uncanny knack for sifting things to get to the basic truth, knew or suspected just what actually had happened in the shack. If only she had called him an out and out liar . . . if she had but blurted out her suspicions . . . how much easier it would have been for Phil. He could have stalked off in high indignation and that doubtless would have been sufficient to cause Nettie to offer a prompt apology. Her silence and her cold, steady eyes followed his every move in the cottage until he had to get away from her. He gave no thought to the fact that by avoiding her at every opportunity he was simply confirming her thoughts and suspicions.

The very first morning after his return home, Phil left the cottage before Nettie awoke. She was surprised to find him gone since she knew how much Phil enjoyed eating a substantial breakfast; still she made no mention of it when he came back that evening. The next morning she pretended she was still asleep when Phil slipped out of bed, caught up his clothes and tiptoed downstairs with them. Peering over the banister rail on the upper floor she watched him dress in the kitchen, saw him let himself out of the cottage. She raced down the stairs after he had gone, watched him from the kitchen window, saw him stride away in the direction of the bunkhouse. It was a comparatively simple matter for her to find out later on that he was making a practice now of snatching a makeshift breakfast of coffee and buns at the bunkhouse. The long hours alone in the cottage gave her imagination added opportunity for wild, unhampered expansion ... but to her credit, when Phil returned for supper, she greeted him with a smile, even permitted him to give her a peck of a kiss on her cheek. She served him his supper, and the layer cake she placed on the table with his coffee was the last word in dessert. But despite her firm resolve and determination, Nettie proved she was only human.

As usual, when Phil finished eating, he opened his belt and the top button of his pants, pushed his chair back from the table, sank back in it and closed his eyes. Nettie watched him out of the corner of her eye.

'Anything happen today?' she asked with studied and rehearsed casualness as she began to clear the table.

Phil opened his eyes.

'Huh? Nope, nothing outta the ord'nary.'

'You're working awf'lly hard these days, aren't you?'

He shrugged his shoulder.

'O-h, I dunno. Still, work never killed 'nybody, y'know.'

'I suppose not.'

He closed his eyes again.

'I was in town today,' she said presently.

'That so?'

'Yes,' she continued. 'I bought this.'

'Huh?' he said and opened his eyes.

'I bought the material for this dress,' she said. 'I made it this afternoon. Do you ... do you like it?'

'Yeah, sure,' he said quickly. 'Looks fine.'

She carried some dishes away from the table, retraced her steps almost immediately.

'I saw Cathy and her sister in town, too,' she went on as she heaped the remaining plates preparatory to removing them from the table.

'Uh-huh.'

'That Gay Hollis woman is a good looking woman.'

This time he made no answer.

'I had a good look at her today,' Nettie continued in her matter-of-fact way of talking. She covered the butter. 'It was really the first good look I've had of her. I think I can understand now why men fall all over her.'

There was still no response, no comment from Phil.

'There's a certain something about her that

seems to attract men to her. It's sort of wide-eyed brazenness, like a challenge. It must be that for every man she passed turned and looked at her. She was wearing a sweater, a green one, and a jacket over it, but after a while she took off the jacket and carried it over her arm. She's actually heavier than you think, and that tight sweater, we-ll . . .'

She rolled up the tablecloth, opened it again over the iron sink and shook the crumbs from the cloth into it, then she folded up the cloth and dropped it into a chair.

'That Corbin man,' she went on again presently. 'The one who runs that saloon, we-ll, he was standing outside his place when Gay came along. Cathy had gone into a store meanwhile. Anyway, Corbin said something to Gay and she smiled and stopped. You'd think they'd met before from the way they just stood there and talked. The next thing I knew, he was leading her into his place and he had his arm around her waist. Cathy came out, saw them going into the saloon, and she put down her packages and ran after them. It wasn't a minute later when Gay and she came out. Cathy was furious. I heard her call Gay a common flirt. Cathy was still telling her what she thought of her as they drove out of town.'

Phil climbed stiffly to his feet.

'Reckon I'll get washed and turn in,' he said. 'Got another full day ahead o' me t'morrow.'

He trudged up the stairs. A door on the upper floor closed behind him presently. Nettie sobbed softly, wiped her eyes with the corner of a dish towel, then she seemed to square her shoulders and started washing the dishes.

★   ★   ★

Supper in the big house was a quiet affair with practically no conversation among the three people who sat at the kitchen table. When the meal was finished, Gay got to her feet and went upstairs; she returned shortly with her coat over her arm. Cathy had started to clear away the dishes ... she stopped and looked up at Gay who donned her coat, and buttoned it up.

'I'm just going for a short stroll,' Gay said in answer to Cathy's unasked question. 'I think a breath of air will do me good.'

Cathy gathered the dishes together ... the door closed behind Gay. George got up from the table.

'Too much to expect her t' give you a hand with the dishes?' he asked.

Cathy smiled at him.

'O-h, I don't mind doing them by myself,' she replied. 'Besides, Gay isn't the domesticated kind, you know.'

'Isn't she?' he asked. 'What'd she do 'bout dishes and things when she was livin' with 'er

93

husband?'

'That was different,' Cathy said a bit lamely.

'Yeah,' he said. 'I'll bet it was.'

He hitched up his pants, caught up his hat and slapped it on his head and stalked out. Again the door closed shut. He sauntered away from the house, glanced in the direction of the bunkhouse as he came abreast of it, then he quickened his pace. He was probably a hundred yards from the house when he spied a slim figure ahead of him.

'There she is, awright,' he muttered to himself. 'Wonder where she's headed for?'

He swerved toward a fringe of trees, lengthened his stride in an effort to overtake her. In the protective shadows of the trees he broke into a trot. He saw Gay turn off toward the road that led to town.

'Must be expectin' someb'dy out fr'm town,' he decided.

Now he permitted her to increase the gap between them ... when he was satisfied that she had reached the roadside, he swung wide, circling her, and finally panted up to the road, too, though probably fifty feet beyond the spot where she was waiting. It was less than five minutes later when he heard the clatter of approaching hoof beats. He peered into the road, hastily backed against a nearby tree when a horseman loped up, whirled past him. The hoof beats slowed, then they stopped altogether. George grunted, hitched up his belt and trudged up the road. He heard the gentle whinny of a horse in the darkness ahead of him ... suddenly he saw the horse, and two figures standing beside the animal. They sprang apart. George stopped.

'Awright, Gay,' he said curtly. 'Reckon you c'n turn around now and trot back home.'

'Just a minute,' her companion said. It was Corbin.

'O-h, so it's you again, eh? Thought I told you t' stay off the Circle-A?'

'This isn't the Circle-A,' Corbin answered coldly. 'This is a public road.'

'Yeah, s'ppose it is. But she ain't public property, so get goin'.'

'You're taking a lot on yourself, aren't you?' Corbin retorted. 'I think this lady is quite capable of deciding whether she wants to see me or not, without your help.'

'Long as she lives on my place, I'll help 'er decide the things I think she needs help in. Get goin', Mister, before I help you get started.'

'Perhaps you'd better go,' the slim figure that was Gay said.

Corbin was silent and motionless for a moment, then he shrugged his broad shoulder.

'All right,' he said heavily. 'I'll go. But one of these days, Akers...'

'I know, I know,' George said, interrupting

him. 'Seems t' me that was the same spiel you gave me the last time you were here. You oughta change it, or mebbe you oughta just wait f'r that day you're allus talkin' about and then start chirpin'.'

Corbin moved toward his horse.

'Just so you don't get 'ny fool ideas, Mister, once you get up on your horse, you might r'member that I got my hand wrapped aroun' my gun butt.'

Corbin swung up into the saddle. He wheeled his horse and rode swiftly down the shadow-draped road. Presently his horse's pounding hoof beats faded out. Gay turned on her heel and started up the road ... George followed at her heels. They were nearly in sight of the house when he stepped up beside her. She looked at him, halted in the middle of the road. He stopped too.

'Look, Gay,' he began. 'It ain't f'r me or f'r anybody else t' try t' tell you what you c'n do or what you cain't do. Heck, you're old enough to know what's right and what ain't right f'r y'self.'

'O-h, thank you!'

He disregarded her tone of sarcasm.

'I just don't like any messin' around. You know what I mean, so cut it out. 'Course, if you ain't got 'ny respect f'r y'self, that's somethin' else again, but then you might think o' your sister. She's got a good name 'round these parts and I don't aim t' let anyone spoil it for 'er, not even you. That clear?'

'I'm sure my sister will be deeply touched when I tell her of your fears for her reputation.'

'There's just one thing more,' George continued. 'You heard me tell it to Corbin. Long's you live on the Circle-A, you're gonna behave y'self or you're gonna get the hell off it. This is the last time I'm gonna mention it, Gay. If you don't cut out this messin' around, I'm just gonna tell you t' pack up and get goin', and that'll be that, b'lieve me.'

She pushed past him, started away, but he reached out, caught her by the arm and halted her.

'I hadn't intended mentionin' this, but long's you're gonna act nasty 'bout things, here goes. This carryin' on with Phil Martin ...'

'Yes?'

'I'm givin' you just one warnin'. Stay away fr'm Phil. Understand?'

'Aren't you letting your jealousy run away with you, Mister Akers?'

'Huh? My what?'

'Your jealousy! I think you're jealous of Phil. But I don't blame you for being jealous of him. He's a man. That's more than I can say for you!'

George stiffened. He pushed her aside roughly, strode up the road.

97

'I hate you!' she screamed. 'If you think you're going to run my life, you've another thought coming! You ... you...!'

George simply quickened his pace, turned in the direction of the bunkhouse, disappeared in the enveloping night light. Gay stumbled along, sobbing brokenly. A shadowy figure stepped out of the brush, halted in the road. Gay, her head bent, collided with him, backed away from him in fright.

'Gay, honey, what's the matter?'

She stared at him for a brief moment.

'Phil!' she sobbed and threw herself in his arms. 'Phil!'

He held her tightly, patted her head and back clumsily but gently.

'Phil,' she whispered. 'Take me away from here!'

He held her off at arm's length, eyed her questioningly.

'What's happened?'

'O-h, nothing,' she answered. 'It's just that, we-ll, I've simply got to get away from here. I can't stand it any longer. I feel like a prisoner. My soul isn't my own here.'

'Oh!' he said. He knew his reply was inadequate, that he should have said something more sympathetic, yet his voice reflected his relief over the fact that there wasn't anything radically wrong, and finally, he decided, she was probably being emotional

98

as women like to be. His hands released their grip on her shoulders.

She looked up at him.

'Phil, you want me, don't you?'

'Do you hafta ask me that? Don't you know?'

'Then do something about it,' she pleaded. She clung to him now. 'Phil, take me away from here, please! Anywhere at all, California, or any place you choose, just so long as we get away from here.'

'Yeah, sure,' he said but his answer was slow and hesitant. Phil had always been like that. One planted an idea in him, gave him time to think about it before he could give an answer or wax enthusiastic about it. But this time the idea took hold promptly. 'Sure, honey, sure. The on'y thing is I ain't got 'ny money right now. We'll hafta wait a while, then mebbe in . . .'

'Then get the money!'

'Gay, honey . . .'

She broke away from him.

'All right,' she sobbed. 'I'll get someone else to take me away from here. Someone who really wants me, someone who'll be glad to have me!'

She whirled past him, fled up the night-black, shadowy road. He stared after her fleeing figure; when she had disappeared from sight, he shook his head sadly. He turned wearily, pushed through the brush again, trudged away. He swung wide around the cottage to the rear, peered through the kitchen window. Nettie was asleep at the table, her head pillowed in her folded arms. Stealthily, Phil let himself in . . . he bolted the door, inched his way past the table to the stairs, crept up the single flight safely to the bedroom, undressed and climbed into bed. It was probably an hour later when Nettie came upstairs. The light in the lamp on the bureau blazed fully and yellowishly; Phil hadn't bothered to dim it. Nettie went to it at once, lowered it, then she tiptoed around the bed. Phil was fast asleep. He lay on his side, his face to the wall. She bent down, peered into his face, studied it for a moment, wondered what he was dreaming about. When he stirred, she moved away hastily.

She undressed presently, donned her nightgown, turned her head and looked at Phil when he grunted and slipped over on his back. She turned out the lamp light, got into bed. The bed sheets were cold and she moved over toward Phil. He stirred again and his heavy arm slid across her body. She did not push it off . . . instead she lay very still beneath it for a moment, then she moved a bit closer to him. His arm seemed to tighten around her and she responded eagerly, squirmed over on her side, facing him. Her own arm whipped out of the covers, crept upward over his chest.

'Phil,' she whispered.

He grunted, twisted over on his side again. She lay still for another moment, hopefully, then alone again, she turned over on her side, burrowed deep into the blankets. Tears welled up into her eyes, ran down her cheeks and dampened her pillow and nightdress. She sobbed softly, stifling it by burying her face in the pillow. Nettie finally cried herself to sleep. In the morning, when she awoke, Phil was gone. She got out of bed, dressed and went downstairs. She moved slowly, almost listlessly, in a manner that was unusual for her. She heard voices outside and she raised her head ... she went to the window that opened on the big house and peered out. Midway between the cottage and the house were three men, Phil, George Akers and a third man, a man with a thin face and white hair. Nettie was certain she had never seen him before. She raised the window an inch or two.

'Like I said before, Snediker,' she heard George say. 'I'm willin' to do business on that herd I got in the north pasture, but I don't aim t' give them four hundred head o' cattle away. What's your proposition?'

'Seventy-five hundred bucks, cash,' the white-haired man said in a gruff voice. 'Take it or leave it.'

'I'm leavin' it,' George said coldly. 'You don't wanna buy cattle, Mister. You wanna steal 'em.'

Snediker whipped out a roll of bills. He waved it under George's nose.

'What'n hell does that look like?' he demanded angrily. 'You danged fool you oughta be tickled t' death that I'm offerin' t' pay you anything. In another couple o' weeks them head o' cattle won't be yourn t' give away, much less t' sell.'

'Maybe.'

'Maybe, nuthin'! I got seventy-five hundred bucks in this roll. Get busy and write me out a bill o' sale and the money's yourn. My men'll be here this afternoon t' drive the cattle over t' my place.'

'Not interested, Snediker.'

The cattleman turned to Phil.

'Martin,' he said. 'You're foreman o' this half-baked outfit. You must know somethin' about cattle an' things, or you wouldn't have the job. Think you c'n talk some sense into this danged fool?'

Phil grinned and shook his head.

'He's got all the sense he needs, Snediker,' he said. 'You know same's we do that seventy-five hundred is just half what that herd's worth.'

Snediker glared at him, shoved the roll into his pants pocket.

'What it's worth an' what you c'n get f'r it are two diff'rent things alt'gether,' he snapped. 'Wa-al, what'll it be? Do we do business, or don't we?'

'You c'n have that herd f'r ten thousand bucks,' George said with finality. 'Even that's almost givin' 'em away, but bein' that I c'n use the money, I'm willin' t' take a little loss on the deal.'

'I'll make it eight thousand,' Snediker answered. 'But that's as high as I'll go.'

George hitched up his belt. He turned to Phil.

'I'm goin' in and have s'me breakfast,' he said. 'You had yourn already?'

'No,' Phil replied. 'I'll get me a cup o' coffee down at the bunkhouse and get goin'. I got things t' do.'

George nodded, turned on his heel and strode into the house. The kitchen door slammed behind him. Snediker followed him with his eyes.

'Danged fool,' he muttered.

Phil grinned again.

'George is awright,' he said. 'Mebbe he don't know as much as you do 'bout ranchin' and cattle raisin', but he ain't dumb by a helluva long shot. C'mon, I'll walk you down t' the corral. You left your horse there, didn't you?'

Snediker mumbled something under his breath. He gave his pants belt a vicious, angry tug, and trudged away at Phil's side. Nettie watched them swing past the house, then they swerved from sight. Slowly she

103

lowered the window.

CHAPTER SEVEN

BLOOD ON THE SUN

Phil Martin and John Snediker marched along in silence. They had almost reached the corral gate when Phil turned to the cattleman.

'You got a lotta ridin' ahead o' you b'fore you get back t' your place,' he said. 'How 'bout havin' some hot coffee with me b'fore you get goin'?'

Snediker considered briefly.

'Wa-al,' he said finally. 'Awright. Fact o' the matter is, Martin, I ain't had a thing yet t'day. Didn't wait f'r breakfast 'cause I wanted t' get over here fast's I could, not knowin' whether I'd find Akers still here if I took too much time.'

'Come on then,' Phil said. He nodded toward the bunkhouse. 'Over there.'

They entered the bunkhouse to find that a fresh pot of coffee had just been put on the fire. One of the punchers arose from his chair, swung it around.

'Here,' he said to Phil. 'Snediker c'n have it. I don't want it. I've been sittin' around so danged much uv late, I'm gettin' me a backside like a steer's.'

104

Snediker accepted the chair with a brief nod of thanks. Phil watched the coffee pot for a moment.

'One o' you fellers see that Mister Snediker gets 'imself some coffee,' he said. 'I'll come back f'r mine later on.'

'Oughta be ready in another couple o' minutes,' a second puncher said. 'Can'tcha wait that long?'

'Save me some,' Phil answered. 'I'll be back soon.'

He nodded to Snediker, strode out of the bunkhouse, went back to the corral and saddled his horse. Minutes later he rode out of the enclosure and clattered away in a westerly direction. A couple of punchers loped up, nodded to him, swung off toward the bunkhouse. Phil nudged his horse with his knees and the animal quickened his pace. Presently they were going downhill and the ranch buildings fell away behind them. Phil spurred his horse, sent him racing ahead. But after a mile or so, Phil suddenly pulled up, twisted around in the saddle and looked back. When he was evidently satisfied that he was unobserved, he swerved his horse in a southerly direction, sent him pounding away. Mile after mile flashed away behind the horse's thundering hoofs. The early morning sun was bright and warm now and the range grass and tiny sprays of wild flowers filled the air with a pleasant perfume. It was probably an hour later when Phil checked his mount, slowed him to a canter. Directly ahead of them was a hill ... they went up its grassy slope at an easy gait, topped the crest and rode part way down the other side. Phil reined in, dismounted, jerked his rifle out of the saddle boot. He trudged up the hill to its very top, took off his hat and dropped it in the grass, then he sprawled out on his stomach with his rifle at his elbow. From where he lay he commanded a view of miles and miles of the open range. In the distance, westward again, lay the Circle-A. He scanned the countryside carefully, studied every movement and billow of dust. His lips tightened suddenly. In the distance he spied a lone horseman.

'Reckon that's him,' he said half aloud.

He reached for the rifle, realized it would take Snediker half an hour to come within rifle range and he checked himself. The minutes passed slowly ... actually they seemed never ending. Phil's hands were wet with sweat now ... he wiped them on his shirt, reached for the rifle a second time, gripped it, pulled back the bolt. Satisfied that the weapon was loaded, he slid the bolt down again. Snediker was less than half a mile away now. Phil steadied himself ... it would never do to fire too soon. He forced himself to wait, then as he watched with sweat-filled eyes and pounding heart, Snediker came riding up to the foot of the hill. Phil's hands tightened around the rifle, and he raised it halfway to his shoulder, checked himself as before. The cattleman's horse started up the slope. There was a sudden distraction overhead, a frightening sound, and what he thought was the chattering of human voice. His nerves were already on edge, and this brought him close to disaster. His head jerked back, and he looked skyward. He was startled to see a huge black bird come swooping down out of the morning sky, saw it hurtle earthward with breath-taking speed. It seemed to be diving straight at him and he threw up one arm as though to ward it off . . . in another moment the huge bird was past him and he sagged limply.

There was a sudden warning sound on the other side of the hill, a creaking of Snediker's saddle, and it jolted him into consciousness, brought him back to the sordid business at hand. He twisted around again, discovered that Snediker was barely twenty feet from the top of the hill. Actually the cattleman was little more than a blurred vision in the eyes of the man who waited to kill him. The rifle seemed to jerk upward. It roared suddenly, deafeningly, and the peaceful, sunny silence of the range was shattered. Everything was strangely hushed, and the echoing thunder of the rifle lingered in the air. Rifle smoke enveloped Phil . . . it seemed to curl around him, then it began to lift gently. He gulped, peered down at Snediker. The cattleman lay sprawled out on his face, one arm outflung, the other arm bent under his body. His hat lay just beyond him. His horse had stopped ... he turned his head and he looked at his master with an expression of surprise in his brown eyes. He moved, nudged Snediker but there was no response.

Phil got up on his knees. He stared at the outsprawled body; slowly he climbed to his feet, then with the rifle half raised in his clammy hands, he started down the hill. He halted abruptly when he thought Snediker had moved ... after a momentary wait, when he decided that it had simply been an illusion, he went on again. Slowly and cautiously he advanced. There was a curious awkwardness about him ... his legs and feet seemed to be leaden, almost reluctant to move. He stopped a second time, when he came to within a few feet of the prone rancher.

He shifted his rifle, gripped the butt with both hands, then using the weapon as one would use a heavy stick, poked Snediker with the muzzle. Snediker did not move. Phil stepped closer to him, bent over him, then touching him gingerly, turned him over on his back. John Snediker was dead. There was a black-rimmed bullet hole squarely between his sightless eyes. Fresh sweat broke out on Phil's face and hands. He put down the rifle, moved it away from Snediker's outflung hand, knelt down in the grass, and put his own hand into the cattleman's pants pocket. When Phil arose a moment later, Snediker's roll of bills was clutched in his damp hand. Quickly he shoved the wad into his own pocket. He bent over Snediker again, braced himself, then with a mighty effort, hauled the dead man to his feet, and swung him up on his broad shoulder. Slowly he carried him up the hill ... the grass was dewy wet and once or twice Phil slipped and went down on his knees, clinging doggedly to his burden with both hands. But each time he got up again and went on. He stopped presently, to shift the inert body on his shoulder. When the riderless horse finally came alongside, Phil grabbed the bridle and stopped the horse. With an effort that left him breathless, he swung Snediker onto the back of his own mount. The dead man promptly fell forward in the saddle.

Phil eyed him for a moment, then deciding that Snediker wouldn't fall out, wheeled and ran down the hill, caught up his rifle; suddenly remembering that Snediker's hat had fallen off, snatched it up, too. He panted up the hill again, jammed the hat down on the rancher's head, gripped the bridle of his horse and led him over the top of the hill, then down the other side to where Phil's horse was waiting. He returned the rifle to the saddle boot, then, as a precautionary measure, Phil used his own lariat to lash Snediker's body to his horse. He swung himself up astride his own horse, drew the rancher's mount alongside, then rode down the hill.

Curiously enough, now that the deed was done, Phil suddenly discovered that he was completely calm. There was no explaining it, no understanding it. Oddly, too, he had no feel of regret or remorse. Actually he gave no thought to what he had done ... he had needed money, Snediker had had it. It was the simplest kind of a problem; the answer was equally simple. There was nothing personal about the killing, despite the fact that it was the first time that Phil had ever shot a man. Snediker had simply represented the means to the end ... money. That there might be consequences to the man's murder, we-ll, Phil's thoughts did not run along those lines. He thought of one thing only, and that was of Gay Hollis. There wasn't room for anything else in his mind.

When they reached the level of the far-spreading range-land, Phil guided both horses southward. They covered a mile, two miles, then they came to a gully. Phil had discovered the spot some time before. It was a rather odd sort of a place, a gully that had been dry for a long, long time. It was about ten feet long, but it wasn't particularly wide, probably less than a foot in width. It was a spot that most people wouldn't have noticed; those who did, probably paid little or no attention to it, and forgot about it shortly after. Phil dismounted, untied Snediker's body, and let it crash to the ground. The dead man's hat fell off again and Phil simply kicked it into the gully. He dragged Snediker to the spot, rolled him over with his foot, then he bent down and pushed the lifeless body down into the crevice. There were some rocks and stones lying about and Phil covered the body with them. When he straightened up minutes later, he nodded approvingly ... John Snediker was gone. There wasn't a trace of him. Of course there was Snediker's horse to be disposed of and Phil eyed the animal for a moment. The horse looked at him, then as if he sensed what Phil was thinking about, shied away from him. He turned, finally, and jogged away. Phil picked up a rock and hurled it at the animal ... the horse swerved at the right moment and the rock landed far beyond him. Phil promptly forgot about him; he picked up the lariat, coiled it and slung it over his saddle horn, then he mounted his horse and rode away in the direction of the Circle-A.

From time to time he thrust his hand into his pants pocket, just to make sure that Snediker's money was still there. He had never had very much money in his life ... now he felt that he could buy anything he wanted, even the earth. Once or twice he drew out the roll of bills, eyed it, turned it over in his hand, smiled to himself and returned it to his pocket. The range was bright and sunny, he suddenly noticed; he even noticed sprays of wild flowers here and there, eyed them as he had never looked at them before. Then Gay came into his thoughts and he forgot about everything else. Gay with her warm eager lips, her white throat. His thoughts went back to the stormy night in the line rider's shack. He knew he would never forget that night. His horse slowed to a jog presently, finally stopped altogether. Phil suddenly looked up. There was the shack, almost directly ahead of them. A horse was idling in front of the shack, too, and Phil eyed it with surprise. He nudged his mount and they clattered up to the shack. The door opened as they pulled up. Framed in the doorway was Gay Hollis.

'Mornin',' Phil said.

'Good morning,' Gay answered.

Phil eased himself in the saddle, pushed his hat up from his eyes. There was another moment's silence ... their eyes met for a moment, then Gay who seemed unusually quiet and subdued, averted hers, finally looked away.

'Kinda early f'r you to be up and doin',' he said shortly. 'Ain't it?'

'O-h,' she said without looking at him. 'I

112

had a headache when I awoke, so I decided to pass up breakfast in favor of some fresh air.'

'Get 'ny sleep last night?'

'N-o,' she admitted. 'Not too much.'

'That's what I figgered.'

He climbed down from his horse. His mount promptly moved past him, nosed up to Gay's horse, and stopped there. Phil sauntered up to the door. Gay raised her head.

'Still so set on leavin' the Circle-A?' he asked with a smile.

'More so than ever.'

He laughed, hitched up his pants.

'Let's go inside,' he said. 'Got somethin' to talk to you about.'

'Can't we talk out here?'

He smiled again, a curious, meaningful smile, and shook his head. Gay looked at him, questioningly, turned without further delay; Phil followed her inside, closed the door behind him, leaned back against it. Gay stood by the table.

'So you're still set on hightailin' it,' he repeated.

'Yes.'

'When would you like t' go?'

'I'd go this very minute,' she answered, then she added, with a wan smile, 'if I could.'

'How 'bout t'night? That be too late?'

Her eyes probed his face, then eagerness brought her forward.

'Phil,' she said breathlessly. 'You ... you didn't ...'

He laughed, softly this time. He had evidently hoped for this moment, and now that it had materialized, he was enjoying it to the fullest.

'And how I did!' he said. He dug into his pocket, yanked out the roll of bills. 'What's that look like, huh?'

She threw her arms around him, held him tightly.

'Phil!' he heard her say. 'Phil, you great big darling!'

She raised her head and he kissed her on the mouth. He shoved the thick wad of bills into her hands. She was the Gay of old, bright and eager-eyed. She went to the table, started to count the money.

'There's more'n enough in that roll,' he said and she laughed happily. 'Oughta be seventy-five hundred bucks there, mebbe even eight thousand.'

He came up behind her, wrapped his great arms around her, buried his face in her hair.

'Happy?' he asked.

'Oh, yes!' she replied. She turned around in his arms. 'Phil, let's go to California.'

She smiled up at him.

'Please!'

He grinned boyishly, bent his head and kissed the tip of her nose.

'Awright,' he said. 'Anywhere you like.'

She handed him the money, watched him shove it into his pants pocket, then she stepped back, pushed a stray strand of hair back into place. He looked at her ... there was a curious smile on his face.

'Why are you looking at me like that?' she asked.

He turned away slowly, halted when he reached the bunk, looked down at it, then he turned to face her again.

'Ain't you even curious t' know where I got all that dough,' he said, 'after telling you last night that I didn't have any?'

'I knew you had it. You were just testing me. That's all.'

'Oh,' he said.

'I'd better start back,' she said. 'Cathy will be wondering if I don't get back shortly.' She turned toward the door. 'Bye, darling.'

'Wait a minute,' he said and she stopped, looked at him over her shoulder.

'Yes, Phil?'

He strode across the shack floor to the door, stood with his shoulders against it.

'I think you oughta know where I got that dough,' he said quietly.

'O-h, Phil, must we go into that now? Can't we talk about it some other time? It's getting late, you know, and I don't want Cathy to get suspicious and spoil things for us.'

'Gay, I killed a man this mornin'. That

115

dough I got in my pocket is his. Leastways, it was his.'

She stared at him with widening eyes, then the color drained out of her face when the full impact of what he had just said struck her.

'No!' she gasped. 'You didn't! You're teasing me, testing me again!'

She backed away from him, collided with the table, moved, then swerving, followed it until she was behind it.

'I'm tellin' you the truth, Gay,' Phil said. 'I'd rather have you hear it fr'm me 'stead o' gettin' it fr'm somebody else.'

She stared at him, then a sob escaped her ... her mother's face flashed into her thoughts, then she heard her mother's voice.

'Gay,' her mother said. 'No good will ever come of you. Mark my words.'

Gay screamed. She whirled around the table, struck at Phil ... he backed away from her although he made no attempt to defend himself despite the knowledge that he had but to put out his hand to keep her off.

'You fool!' she screamed. 'You fool! You great big clumsy fool! I wouldn't have any part of you if you had a million dollars, all your own, too! Go back to your precious Nettie! I don't want you!'

His arm flashed up, and he slapped her across the mouth ... she staggered away from him, fell against the table ... she came erect almost immediately. There was a tiny speck

116

of blood at the corner of her mouth. She squared her slender shoulders.

'Open the door, please,' she said.

He turned slowly, gripped the door knob . . . he was motionless for a moment, then he twisted the knob and the door opened. He turned again, held the door open wide. Gay stormed past him, out of the shack. He filled the open doorway with his bulk. His jaw muscles twitched but no word fell from his tightened lips. He watched her mount her horse, saw her whirl the animal around and send him racing away. Phil sagged brokenly . . . he turned and disappeared into the shack. The door closed of its own accord. Gay was probably a hundred yards from the shack when a pistol shot shattered the morning air. She jerked her mount to a stop, twisted around in the saddle and looked back. She sobbed again, openly, pulled her horse around and dashed back to the shack. She pulled up at the door, slid out of the saddle, ran to the door and flung it open.

'Phil!' she sobbed as she burst in. She stopped in her tracks and stared hard with fear-widened eyes. 'Phil!'

There was no response from Phil Martin. He lay on the shack floor, a big awkwardly sprawled-out hulk of a man, his left arm doubled up under him, his right arm outflung. Clutched in his right hand was his Colt. Gay pressed her clenched fist to her mouth to stifle the scream that arose in her throat.

'Phil!' she whispered. 'Phil!'

She tiptoed around the table, peered down at him. There was a widening pool of blood under him. She backed away hastily, stopped again presently. She frowned ... she was evidently debating something. Then she moved toward him again, swiftly and purposefully. She bent over him a second time, put her hand into his pants pocket. She straightened up shortly, thrust the roll of bills into her sweater, then she wheeled and went out. She retraced her steps, pulled the door shut, ran to her horse, mounted him, sent him racing away.

CHAPTER EIGHT

MURDER WILL OUT

Once a month, generally about the middle of the month it was the custom of Sheriff Buck Loomis to 'inspect' the county. It was a word of Buck's own choosing, a word that helped lend an air of official importance to his cross-county jaunts. Actually there was little need for an inspection ... the county was spanned by big ranches whose hired hands were usually kept well occupied, and thus, possessed of little time for trouble making, made Sheriff Loomis' life quite bearable. There were ample grazing grounds, plenty of water, and the usual quarrels that abounded in the average cattle raising county were missing here. Still, Buck persisted in his inspections even though everyone knew they were just social calls, a means of breaking the monotony of town life. At the same time, the ranchers looked forward to Buck's visits. Hospitality demanded that they devote some time to entertaining him and they were always glad of the opportunity to break away from their every day responsibilities. Buck was a source of news to them. He always brought with him the latest news from town as well as news from the ranches he had already visited.

For instance, the curious antics of Gabe Foster, the owner of the Diamond-Dot ranch, were always a source of merriment to the other ranchers. Gabe was always doing something, something that always delighted the rest of the county. Buck had the latest Foster story ready for recital. Gabe, it developed, had just become a grandfather. In his eagerness to celebrate the event, Gabe neglected to notice that the label on the jug he picked up read 'vinegar.' A jug was a jug to him, labels or no, so it was doubtful if he would have bothered to read the label even if he had noticed it. Gabe, who was known to drink and swallow before he tasted anything, drank a full tumbler of vinegar before he realized that he had made a mistake. It was only afterward that he discovered the whiskey jug on the floor beside his favorite chair. A huge swallow of whiskey seemed to have become embroiled with a like quantity of vinegar ... the tempest in his stomach refused to subside for nearly a week. When it did, Gabe was so worn out from his sudden and frenzied dashes to the outhouse that he took to his bed to regain his lost strength.

Jack Benson, a veteran hand on the Dot-O-Dot was another favorite. Buck reported that Jack had met with something of an accident. There were immediate expressions of sympathy, and equally insistent demands that Buck tell them more. Jack, he related, had dozed off in his bunk with a half-smoked cigarette clutched in his hand. He had awakened to find the bunk, the bunkhouse and himself on fire. In a frantic dash to escape from what appeared then might become his own funeral pyre, Jack dived through the bunkhouse window. Unfortunately someone had neglected to inform Jack that after some eight or ten months of being without a windowpane, a new pane had just been installed in the gaping window frame. Mike Brady, Jack's employer for more than twenty years, was very much annoyed over the incident ... not so much by Jack's burns, cuts or bruises, but over the loss of Jack's services during round-up time which was almost upon them. Jack was very much put out, too. Brady had docked him for the time needed for recuperation, and for the cost of the glass, plus the transportation charges.

Of interest too to the ranchers was the news that a new general store had been opened in town. The appearance of a newcomer always aroused interest.

On these jaunts, Loomis was generally accompanied by his first deputy, lanky, red-headed Pat McCabe. Loomis was an untiring talker, while McCabe was the listener type. Loomis, it was said, could talk from sunup to sundown; Pat, it was reported, could listen to him with apparent interest as long as Buck talked. No one seemed able to understand how Pat endured Buck's repeated recitals of his days as a cattleman, or of his earlier life as a lawman when he was pressed into service to 'take over' for his father who was then Sheriff of a small border town, and who was bedridden at the time as the result of a gunshot wound suffered in a brief encounter with a band of rustlers. Buck always liked to tell how he recruited a party of vigilantes who looked to him, evidently because of his father, for guidance. Buck, according to his story, led an attack on a shack in which the rustlers had holed up, then with two Colts in his hands, he burst in the door, plunged into

121

the shack and trading shot for shot with the outlaw leader, blasted him to death. The other rustlers, incidentally, were hung on the spot. Sometimes Buck neglected to mention this final detail ... that was probably due to the fact that he was too busy to be bothered with a hanging.

'Seems like I'll never be able to f'rget that day,' Buck mused as they rode along. 'You'd think it was on'y yesterday when it happened 'stead o' nearly thirty years ago. It's funny, y'know, how some things kinda stick in a feller's mem'ry.'

'Yeah,' Pat said. 'Ain't it though? But what beats me, Buck, is that you didn't hold back, not even f'r a single minute, even though you knew all along that them fellers were killers.'

Buck laughed softly, modestly, just as he had done so many times before after the same recital, and in response to the same remark Pat had made so many times before. As always, too, Pat grinned and shook his head.

'Doggoned good thing,' he said, 'that you didn't stop to think o' what you were doin' or mebbe you wouldn'ta done it.'

Buck always grew grave when Pat said that. 'O-h, I dunno about that, Pat,' he said. 'Y'know, when a feller's gotta do somethin', reckon he just goes ahead and does it.'

Pat considered for a moment.

'Yeah, I suppose that's right.'

A brief period of silence always followed

... it gave Buck a chance to commune with his memories. He looked up with surprise when McCabe jerked his horse to a sudden stop, pulled up, too, much to the annoyance of his own mount.

'S'matter?' Buck demanded.

'See that horse over there?' McCabe asked, pointing.

Loomis followed Pat's finger, then he nodded.

'Uh-huh. What about 'im?'

'He's saddled and on the loose. Wonder where 'is rider is?'

Buck eyed the animal.

'He must be somewhere's around.'

'Yeah, sure, but how come 'is horse hightailed it?'

They sat in silence for the next minute ... the riderless horse finally raised his head and whinnied shrilly. Buck straightened up in his saddle.

'Come on,' he said and loped forward. Pat followed at arm's length. They rode up to where the other horse waited, then the animal turned and trotted away. Buck and Pat looked at each other. The horse stopped again and looked back. 'What'n blazes d'you make o' that?'

'Looks to me,' Pat observed 'that he's tryin' t' tell us somethin'.'

They spurred their mounts, clattered up to the third horse ... again he wheeled and jogged off.

'I got 'n idea he wants us to follow 'im,' Buck said.

'That's just what I'm thinkin',' Pat said and Buck frowned.

Again they rode after the other horse . . . they loped southward for a time, then, still following, they went down an incline and pulled up when their 'guide' stopped near a gully.

'So what?' Pat asked.

Buck rubbed his nose.

'Don't ask me,' he replied. He twisted around in the saddle. 'Don't see 'nybody. Do you?'

'Nope.'

Buck swung himself out of the saddle. Pat followed suit. Together they trudged over to the gully, peered down. Buck stiffened suddenly.

'S'matter?' McCabe demanded. 'What'd you see?'

'Blood,' the Sheriff answered. 'Come on.'

This time the horse did not turn and move away when they came up to him. He backed the barest bit and whinnied . . . Pat rubbed the horse's nose as he stepped around him. Buck caught him by the arm, and Pat froze in his tracks. Buck pointed to the ground. There was a trail of blood and they followed it silently. A minute later they found the body of John Snediker.

It was about four o'clock that afternoon when Sheriff Loomis, Deputy McCabe and a third man, a stockily-built man with a leathery face and a thick, sun-bronzed neck that looked like a tree stump, clattered into view from the direction of the road that led to town, cantered past the bunkhouse, glancing fleetingly at a group of Circle-A punchers who were idling in front of it, swerved their mounts and rode off toward the big house. They checked their horses shortly, slowed them to a walk. They heard a door slam and they reined in instantly, and looked up expectantly. George Akers came striding around the house from the rear. He stopped when he saw them . . . at a word from Loomis the three men rode up to him, pulled up directly in front of him.

'Howdy,' the Sheriff said. 'You Akers?'

'That's right,' George answered.

Loomis dismounted . . . at a nod from him Pat and the third man dismounted, too.

'You the Sheriff?' George asked.

Buck flipped his jacket open . . . a silver star that was slightly tarnished was pinned to his shirt front.

'You fellers sure got here in a hurry,' George said. 'Don't think it's more'n an hour since I sent one o' my men t' get you. You musta traveled some.'

Loomis and McCabe looked at each other.

'You sent f'r us, eh?' Buck mused. 'Why?'

'Didn't my man tell you?'

'Didn't see 'im,' Loomis said simply. 'We come across country an' he prob'bly follered the road.'

'Oh,' George said a bit lamely.

'What'd you want us for?' McCabe asked.

George turned to him.

'My foreman, Phil Martin's dead.'

The Sheriff frowned.

'Dead?' he repeated. 'Y'mean somebody killed him?'

'Nope. I think he killed 'imself.'

'What makes you think so?'

'He was sprawled out on his belly with his gun in his right hand. There was a bullet hole in his heart.'

Loomis looked relieved.

'Then he c'n wait,' he said. 'This is my deputy, Pat McCabe.'

George and the red-headed Pat nodded to each other.

'This feller,' Loomis added, turning toward the third man. 'This feller's Joe Hanlon, foreman o' the Snediker outfit.'

George eyed Hanlon.

'Don't tell me your boss sent you over t' make me another offer,' he said with a tight-lipped smile.

There was a grunt from the Sheriff.

'Snediker ain't sendin' anybody f'r anything,' he said curtly. 'He's dead.'

George's eyes widened.

'Hell,' he said quickly. 'He was here on'y this mornin'.'

Loomis grunted again.

'We know that,' he said. 'That's why we're here now.'

'What d'you mean?'

'Wa-al,' Buck began. 'First off, Snediker didn't kill himself.'

There was no comment from George.

'Second, he was robbed.'

'I see,' George said slowly.

'Akers, Snediker came t' see you about buyin' some o' your cattle. He made you 'n offer?'

George nodded.

'He did, and I turned it down.'

'He show you a roll o' bills he had on 'im?'

George nodded a second time.

'He held the roll right under my nose,' he replied. 'I told him his offer was ridiculous. He got mad, yanked out his roll and waved it at me and hollered, "What does that look like, huh?"'

'He say how much he had in the roll?'

'I think he said somethin' about there bein' seventy-five hundred in the roll. When I turned 'im down, he upped his offer to eight thousand even, so I suppose that's what he had there 'stead o' the seventy-five hundred he said at first.'

'Where did all this price talkin' take place?' McCabe asked.

127

George turned and pointed.

'Right over there,' he said. 'Not more'n ten or mebbe fifteen feet fr'm where we're standin' right now.'

'Who was there?' the Sheriff asked. 'Just you and Snediker?'

'Martin was with us.'

'F'r how long?'

'Fr'm the beginnin' right down t' the time we finished talkin'.'

'An' Martin's dead, too,' McCabe mused.

'Akers,' Loomis said. 'I understand Snediker made some threatenin' remarks to you. That right?'

'If he did, I didn't hear 'im.'

'Mebbe it was the other way 'round,' McCabe said.

A frown darkened George's face.

'What's that s'pposed to mean?' he demanded.

McCabe smiled fleetingly.

'That you threatened Snediker,' he said.

George eyed him for a moment.

'Mister,' he said evenly. 'I was on'y knee-high to a grasshopper when I found out that it didn't pay t' go 'round accusin' folks o' things 'less I had somethin' t' back up what I was claimin'. How would you like t' have your teeth kicked down your threat?'

McCabe gulped, swallowed and reddened ... Loomis pushed him aside hastily.

'Just a minute, young feller,' he said.

'Nobody's accusin' you o' anything.'

' 'Course not,' George said cuttingly. 'I just dreamed up the idea.'

'We repr'sent the law,' Loomis continued. 'The law gives us the right t' ask questions.'

'Then ask 'em,' George snapped in reply. 'On'y don't go answerin' your own questions out loud.'

There was a moment's silence ... George and Buck eyed each other, then the latter coughed lightly behind his hand.

'Let's get back t' what we were talkin' about,' Loomis said presently. 'What happened afterwards? Snediker got on his horse and ride away?'

'No,' George answered. 'I went into the house, but I understand that Martin took Snediker over to the bunkhouse f'r some coffee. Seems like it wasn't ready when they got there, so after tellin' some o' the boys t' see to it that Snediker got some when it was ready, Martin left him there and went off. I think he said he couldn't wait and that he'd have some after he got back.'

'Where'd he go in such a sweat?'

George shook his head.

'The boys say he rode eastward, like he was headin' f'r town,' he replied.

'How soon did he get back? B'fore Snediker left?'

'He didn't get back at all.'

'I see,' Loomis said. 'Now where'd you

find Martin?'

'In one o' our line rider's shacks.'

'When?'

'O-h, 'bout two hours ago.'

'What'd you do when you found him?'

'I sent one o' my men back here t' tell his wife, then he went on t' town t' get you.'

'Then you weren't alone when you found 'im, that right?'

'I was all alone when I found 'im,' George answered readily. 'I knew some o' my men were aroun' so I went lookin' f'r th'm and brought them back with me t' the shack.'

'Let's get back t' Snediker. What d'you s'ppose happened to 'im?' the Sheriff asked.

George shook his head.

'I wouldn't know how t' answer that question.'

'Think any o' your men might've had it in f'r him?'

'I dunno anything about that. Why don't you ask th'm?'

'I aim to,' Loomis answered. 'When you found Martin, did you find 'ny money on 'im?'

'Y'mean, did I find Snediker's roll on 'im? No.'

'Did you look t' see if Martin had it on 'im?'

'Nope. Soon's I got back with the boys, we lashed 'im to 'is own horse and brought 'im home.'

130

Loomis rubbed his chin thoughtfully for a moment.

'Why d'you s'ppose Martin killed 'imself?' he asked.

'You've got me there.'

'Did he have 'ny trouble with anyone?'

'Not that I ever heard tell.'

'How 'bout women? Anyone in town he was int'rested in?'

'Martin was married,' George answered. He turned, nodded toward the cottage. Loomis' eyes followed George's. The blind over the kitchen window was drawn to its full length. 'He lived in there, with 'is wife.'

'Uh-huh,' Buck said. 'How's she takin' it?'

'How would you expect her t' take it?' George countered.

'I'm askin' you.'

'Even a lawm'n oughta be able t' answer a question like that.'

Their eyes met and clashed briefly.

'You ever have 'ny trouble with 'im?' Loomis asked shortly.

'Nope.'

'Satisfied with 'is work?'

'Yep.'

'And you still say you can't think uva single reason why he'd kill 'imself.'

'Nope.'

McCabe nudged Loomis and the latter turned his head while the deputy whispered to him.

'You think there's any c'nnection between Snediker's killin',' the Sheriff said, 'and Martin's?'

George shook his head.

'I don't think so,' he replied. 'But that don't prove much.'

Loomis and McCabe held another brief and whispered conference.

'Akers,' the Sheriff began. 'I understand you're kinda up against it, that you need dough, and that you need it pronto. That right?'

'I c'n use ten thousand bucks,' George said quietly. 'If that's what you mean.'

'That dough that Snediker had on 'im woulda done you a heap o' good,' Loomis continued. 'Wouldn't it?'

'What he had woulda done most anybody a heap o' good,' George answered evenly.

'But you more'n most anybody else.'

'Awright, if that's the way you want it.'

'I s'ppose you can prove you didn't leave the ranch till this afternoon.'

'Sure I can.'

Loomis hitched up his pants.

'We'll go have a talk with your men,' he said. 'Don't go 'way. We might want to talk t' you again.'

'I'll be around,' George said curtly.

Loomis and McCabe turned and trudged off; Hanlon, who hadn't said a single word, gave George a questioning glance, then he turned on his heel and trooped away. George, frowning, watched them for a time, saw them walk past the corral, turn off toward the bunkhouse.

'George.'

It was Gay Hollis' voice; he recognized it at once and he turned just as she came up to him.

'George,' she said again. 'I'd like to talk to you.'

'Awright,' he said. 'Go ahead.'

'Can't we go somewhere?'

'Reckon this oughta do f'r anything we gotta talk about.'

'As you like,' she said. 'I couldn't help overhearing your conversation with those men.'

'Don't know that it makes much diff'rence if you or anybody else overheard it.'

'I heard you say you needed money.'

'That ain't a secret.'

'Would five thousand dollars help you?'

'Yeah, I s'ppose it would. Why?'

'I've got that much and I haven't any need for it.'

He eyed her for a moment. She waited for him to answer.

'Where'd you get that much dough?' he asked.

'From my husband,' she replied. 'It's yours for as long as you need it.'

He frowned again.

'What's the idea?' he demanded.

'There aren't any strings to my offer,' she said. 'You've given Cathy and me a home, and this is the way we can repay you.'

'I see,' he said slowly. 'Cathy know anything about this?'

'No. Neither does anyone else.'

'How come you didn't tell 'er?'

'I didn't think it was anyone's business.'

'Oh-huh,' he said. 'Where've you got this dough? In the bank?'

She shook her head.

'No. It's in the house.'

'Hey,' he said quickly. 'That ain't the place t' keep that much dough.'

'I had intended banking it,' she explained. 'Then I decided against it.'

'Why?'

She smiled fleetingly.

'I didn't know how long I'd be staying here.'

'Oh,' he said.

'Will you take it?'

He considered for a moment, then he shook his head.

'No,' he said. 'Not that I ain't grateful t' you f'r offerin' to lend it to me. But, I'd rather not take it.'

She shrugged her slender shoulders.

'That's entirely up to you,' she said calmly. 'I've offered it you and you haven't seen fit to accept it.'

134

'It's awf'lly swell o' you, Gay, and I won't f'rget it.'

She smiled again, turned away.

'Wait a minute,' he said and she stopped, looked at him over her shoulder. He came up to her. 'I wish you'd get it to the bank soon's you can.'

'I suppose it would be safest there.'

'Sure,' he said. 'Y'know, the doggonedest things c'n happen and we've had more'n our share o' them already.'

She went into the house. Minutes later she emerged, smiled at George as she went past him. He followed her with his eyes. He saw her open the corral gate, saw her step into the enclosure. Presently she came out, astride a horse. She settled herself in the saddle, tightened her grip on the reins, and rode away. His eyes shifted ... he had caught a glimpse of three men striding away from the bunkhouse. They swerved presently, headed toward the house. He frowned, hitched up his pants.

'Wa-al,' he muttered. 'This oughta be it.'

CHAPTER NINE

THE SHERIFF KNITS HIS BROWS

The bank was an unpretentious affair, a rather ordinary, even drab-looking establishment that wisely made no claims to anything save its purpose in the community's life. The building in which it was housed was one of nine completely identical buildings ... old timers referred to them as Farley's Folly ... nine equally sorrowful looking structures that stood like obediently quiet children around their mother, four on each side of the bank. Farrell, it was said, used his last dollar in the project ... for years, that is until the town became a town, the nine buildings stood vacant. Farrell, finally convinced that he had wasted his time and money, disposed of his holdings in an 'even up' trade for a gold mine which always showed great promise of fulfilling its owner's hopes but which never actually materialized into anything worthwhile. After Farrell died, his heirs, a couple of easterners whom Farrell despised quite heartily, took over the mine and promptly struck pay dirt. The nine buildings also joined the ranks of profit-makers when California-bound cattlemen and punchers, wearied of the already long trek to the promised land, decided they had gone far enough and settled in the town.

The bank stood on a corner. Completely exposed to the elements, the bank appeared to have aged the fastest and the most. The sun and the rain had obliterated the original coat of white paint which Farrell had bestowed, with his blessings, of course ... now the wooden structure wore a curious mottled brown color that was, as one townsman described it, neither here nor there. Even the sign that hung over the bank's doorway had suffered ... there was a wide gap in the letters that formed the word, 'Bank.' A brief study of it disclosed the fact that the letter 'n' had disappeared. A close-up view of the institution's window revealed a red-bordered placard standing in majestic aloofness in the very middle of the window space; it read, 'Jed Oliver, Owner, President and Manager.'

Jed was alone in the bank. He was a short, chubby man whose thinning hair spanned an almost bald head. The pinkish skin on his head peered through his hair rather limpishly. He toyed with the waxed tips of his mustache, smoothed down his hair gently, thoughtfully, unconsciously curled the ends of his hair around his finger. From time to time he looked down at his left hand ... he wore a huge gold signet ring on his middle finger, and he eyed it admiringly. He polished it regularly by blowing his breath on it, then buffing it by brushing it across his shirt-front.

Jed's eyes ranged upward presently; he frowned when he noticed new cracks in the ceiling, scowled when he noted that the paint was peeling on the walls. The counter behind which he was standing was badly scuffed and marked. There were two small desks against the opposite wall, placed there for the convenience and use of the bank's customers. Both desks were battered, and their surface edges were black-ringed from lighted cigarettes left there by depositors who went on to the counter to complete their business, and who, when they had finished, trooped out without thinking of what they had left behind. Jed shook his head sadly. He came around the counter, sauntered to the open doorway and peered out.

There was little activity on the street at that moment ... it was only when he heard the approaching beat of a horse's hoofs that he looked up with any show of interest. The rider came closer, and Jed's eyes quickened.

'H'm,' he said admiringly. 'H'm!'

Gay Hollis slowed her horse to a walk ... when she guided him toward the bank, Jed gulped, wheeled and started back inside, skidded around the counter. When Gay came in he was busy thumbing through a worn ledger. When he finally looked up he pretended to be surprised to find her standing at the counter ... he smiled at her, closed the ledger and pushed it aside.

'How do you do,' he said.

When he smiled the ends of his mustache seemed to point ceilingward.

'What can I do for you, Miss?' he asked.

He had already decided that she was without doubt the prettiest girl he had ever seen.

'I'd like to deposit some money,' she said.

He smiled again and Gay's eyes followed the tips of his mustache.

'We like people who deposit money with us,' he said. ''Specially when they're pretty.'

He looked down at his ring, turned it over on his finger then he raised his eyes.

'Nice,' he said. 'Isn't it?'

'Very.'

'Set me back one hundred and fifty dollars,' he said. 'Cash.'

'Really?'

'It's solid gold. Understand the feller who owned it b'fore me paid more'n twice that much for it.'

'I wouldn't doubt it.'

He rubbed it on his shirt-front, eyed it admiringly, then he looked at her again.

'Now then, what was it you wanted?' he asked, then he laughed softly. 'O-h, yes ... you want to make a deposit.'

'Please.'

He reached for the ledger, drew it closer,

139

opened it, flipped over some pages, finally found a blank one, then he picked up a pencil.

'Name, please?'

'Hollis,' she answered. 'Gay Hollis.'

He nodded, lowered his eyes reluctantly, wrote her name in the book. The page was finger-marked and he eyed it with a frown, drew a pencil line through her name, and turned the page. He turned half a dozen more before he found a clean one, then he wrote her name at the top.

'Gay Hollis,' he said and looked up again. 'Miss, I suppose?'

'Missus.'

His eyebrows arched.

'I'm a widow,' she said and he seemed relieved.

'How much do you want to deposit?' he asked, poising the pencil above the page.

'O-h, five thousand dollars.'

He entered the amount in one of the columns.

'I'd like it credited to the account of George Akers,' she said suddenly.

'O-h,' he said. 'George Akers, eh?'

'Yes.'

He thumbed through the ledger again, stopped when he came to a page filled with entries.

'Five thousand,' he said and entered it. 'Better take out the page I wrote for you before I find myself out five thousand.'

He flipped the pages over until he came to the one that bore her name, smiled up at her, and ripped it out.

'That's the quickest way,' he said. 'The money, if you please.'

She made no movement ... suddenly he realized there was a neat package of bills on the counter and he smiled again, a bit sheepishly, picked it up and counted it carefully.

'Five thousand it is,' he said. 'Thank you, Mrs. Hollis.'

'Oh,' she said, stopped and looked at him.

'Yes?'

'Does Mr. Akers have to be told who made the deposit for him?' she asked.

'Wh-y, no,' he answered.

'On the other hand,' she said, 'I don't think it will make any difference to him if you do tell him.'

'Doesn't he know anything about this?'

'Oh, yes,' she said quickly and colored. 'He gave it to me for this purpose.'

He eyed her questioningly.

'Then he must know about this, mustn't he?'

'Of course.'

He rubbed his chin with his right thumb. Gay turned toward the door.

'G'bye,' she said: 'And thank you.'

She went out. Jed was motionless. He

looked down at the package of bills, picked it up, hefted it for a moment, turned it over in his hand, finally put it down on the counter. He stiffened suddenly and his eyes widened ... he grabbed the money, came whirling around the counter and burst out of the bank. He stopped in his tracks, barely avoiding a horseman who rode past him ... it was Gay and she twisted around in the saddle and looked back at him. He stared up at her. He watched her for a moment as she clattered away, then he raced down the street, panted into the Sheriff's office. Tod Waters, Loomis' second deputy, was seated at the Sheriff's desk, his booted feet propped up on an opened drawer. Tod looked up.

'Where's the Sheriff?' Jed demanded breathlessly.

'Out.'

'When'll he be back?'

'Soon,' Tod answered and grinned. 'I hope.'

Jed frowned.

'Know where he is?' he asked.

Tod shook his head.

'Nope.'

'We-ll, suppose you had to get him in a hurry. What would you do about it?' Jed demanded.

Tod grinned up at him again.

'Wouldn't do anything,' he replied unruffled. 'Wouldn't know where to look f'r him.'

The frown on Jed's face deepened.

'That's fine,' he said. 'Very fine.'

Tod shrugged his shoulder.

'Mebbe. Still that's the way it is. S-ay, what's this all about, huh? Can't I do anything? Does it hafta be the Sheriff?'

'Will you tell him I want him when he gets back?'

'Yeah, sure,' Tod said. 'And I won't do. That right?'

'I want the Sheriff.'

'I'll tell him soon's I see him.'

Jed wheeled and strode out.

It was an hour or two later when Sheriff Loomis and Deputy McCabe rode into town. Jed reached the doorway when they had passed. He cupped his hands around his mouth and yelled.

'Sheriff!'

The two lawmen looked back . . . when he gesticulated, they looked at each other, wheeled their horses and rode back, pulled up in front of him.

'S'matter, Jed?' Loomis asked.

'Will you come inside a minute, please?'

'Can't it wait?'

'No,' Jed said firmly. 'It's important.'

Buck swung himself out of the saddle.

'Want me, too?' McCabe asked.

'Yeah,' the Sheriff answered. 'Mebbe you'd better sit in on this too, Pat.'

143

McCabe dismounted ... he followed Loomis and Oliver into the bank. Jed went at once to the ledger, opened it.

'See that?' he asked.

'Sure,' Loomis said. 'What's it supposed t' be?'

Jed frowned.

'It's a ledger page,' he said. There was annoyance in his voice. 'It's the account of George Akers.'

'Oh,' Buck said. 'George Akers, eh?'

'Yes,' Jed said. 'See that deposit figure there?'

He pointed to it and both Buck and Pat bent over.

'Five thousand dollars deposited to his credit today,' Oliver said. 'Does that mean anything to you?'

'You're damned tootin' it does,' Loomis said quickly. 'When was he here?'

'He wasn't,' Jed said curtly.

'Then how...?'

'He sent it in.'

'Oh,' the Sheriff said.

'Hey,' McCabe said at his elbow. 'Where'n hell did he get all that dough all uva sudden, huh?'

'That,' Jed said, 'is a question I thought you gentlemen would like to ask him.'

'You say he sent that dough?'

Jed gave McCabe a cold stare.

'Yes,' he said, bridling his impatience. 'A

young woman brought the deposit. A very pretty young woman, too, I might add. A Mrs. Gay Hollis.'

'Never heard o' her,' Pat said.

'She's one o' the Ballard girls,' Sheriff Loomis explained.

'Oh,' McCabe said. 'How'd she come t' that other name?'

It provided an opportunity for a full-hilted thrust and Jed Oliver snatched it up happily.

'Hollis,' he said very stiffly, 'is probably her husband's family name. Women take their husband's last names, y'know, when they marry them. It's done every day, I'm told.'

'No kiddin'?' Pat said sarcastically.

Jed nodded gravely.

'You can take my word for it.'

McCabe turned to the Sheriff.

'Hey, that just about ties things up, don't it? Snediker was killed f'r his dough. Akers owes 'is shirt and he ain't got a dime, then all uva sudden out uva clear sky, he comes up with a whole fistful o' dough.'

'Uh-huh,' Buck said, nodding. 'Mister Akers is where I wouldn't be, headin' f'r a hangin'. Come on, Pat.'

'Huh? Heck, Buck, don't tell me we're...'

Loomis was halfway to the door.

'Buck,' McCabe said protestingly. 'Ain't we even gonna eat b'fore we get goin' again, huh? Besides, I've been waitin' all day to...'

145

'We'll eat afterwards,' the Sheriff flung over his shoulder as he stepped outside.

'Damnation,' McCabe muttered. He hitched up his pants, glared at Jed. 'Did you hafta tell 'im right off? Couldn't you 've waited till t'morrow mornin'?'

Oliver smiled gently.

'I'm a law abiding citizen,' he answered.

'You're somethin' else, too,' Pat said gruffly. 'On'y I ain't got the time now t' stop and tell you. R'mind me of it some other time.'

He stormed out of the bank mumbling to himself.

*　　　*　　　*

It was evening. There was no activity on the Circle-A. Even the usual sound of loud voices floating out through the open window in the bunkhouse was missing ... in the corral the horses seemed strangely hushed, contented to keep to themselves without the usual milling about and the consequent trampling of one another. It was quiet in the kitchen in the big house, too. Gay and George had just seated themselves at the table. Gay having returned from town but minutes before. Cathy moved about in her usual quiet and efficient way. She served Gay, placed George's plate in front of him, brought her own plate to the table and sat down facing them. She picked up her fork, glanced at her sister, then she looked at George.

'You're both awfully talkative tonight,' she remarked.

There was no comment, no reply. Cathy looked at Gay again.

'Gay,' she said, 'what made you go off to town so suddenly?'

Gay did not raise her eyes.

'O-h,' she answered. 'I had something to attend to in town.'

'It must have been terribly urgent.'

'It was,' Gay said and she flushed. 'That is, in a way.'

There was a sudden clatter of hoofs and the three of them looked up as one. George put down his knife and fork. The hoof beats swelled. George did not move again. They heard horses dash past the house. Cathy got to her feet.

'I'd better see who it is,' she said and she went to the kitchen door. She opened it. Two tall figures filled the doorway. 'George,' Cathy said over her shoulder, 'it's the Sheriff.'

Loomis pushed into the kitchen. He glanced at Gay and took off his hat.

'Sorry t' hafta come bustin' in like this,' he said.

George turned slowly in his chair, raised his eyes to meet the Sheriff's.

'S'matter?' he asked and his voice was hard and annoyed. 'Think up some more questions?'

'On'y one,' Loomis replied.

Pat McCabe came inside, too. George glanced at him, but it was only a fleeting glance at best. Pat closed the door behind him, leaned back against it, hooked his thumbs in his gun belt. Cathy moved tableward again ... she crossed the room in front of the Sheriff, halted behind Gay's chair.

'Awright,' George said curtly. 'What's the question?'

Loomis seemed to square his shoulders.

'Akers,' he said, 'I understand you d'posited five thousan' dollars in the bank t'day.'

George's head jerked upward in surprise, but he managed to check and control himself.

'O-h,' he said.

'I'd like t' know where you got that dough,' Buck concluded.

George smiled coldly.

'I borrowed it,' he said and he smiled again, almost tauntingly.

The expression on Loomis' face did not change ... he merely nodded.

'Uh-huh,' he said. 'Mind tellin' me who you borrowed it fr'm?'

'I don't see that that's any o' your bus'ness.'

'Till this Snediker thing is cleared up, everything's my bus'ness,' the Sheriff said sharply. 'I s'ppose you c'n prove you borrowed that five thousan', can'tcha?'

'I don't aim t' prove anything,' George said angrily. 'If you're chargin' me with anything, it's up t' you t' do the provin'.'

Their eyes clashed, but the Sheriff's did not waver.

'Look, Akers,' he said presently. 'I didn't come chasin' all the way out here just f'r the ride. There's been a murder around here, and a robbery, too, and that's doggoned serious bus'ness t' me. Till I know who did the job on Snediker, everybody's a suspect t' me. You're included among 'em. Now why don't you smarten up an' talk? If you borrowed the dough, well an' good, and that's all there'll be t' that, and you'll be in the clear, leastways far's the five thousand's c'ncerned. Now how about it?'

'I've got nothing t' say.'

Sheriff Loomis shrugged his shoulder.

'Y'understand, Akers, that you're actu'lly forcin' me t' take you in, don'tcha?' he asked.

'Sheriff,' Gay said suddenly, and all eyes turned to her.

'Ma'm?'

'The money was mine,' she said quietly.

Color drained out of her face. There was silence in the room for a moment, a strained, oppressive silence. Finally, Loomis coughed lightly behind his hand.

'Uh-huh,' he said. 'I know you d'posited

the money for him, Ma'm. And if as you say, it was your money, why'n thunder couldn't he say so 'stead o' actin' so danged mysterious about it?'

'Because he didn't know anything about it.'

Loomis' eyebrows arched.

'I see,' he said, but it was evident that he didn't see at all, and that he was simply waiting for her to explain.

'I offered to lend it to George,' she went on presently. 'But he refused it.'

'Why?'

Gay shook her head.

'I don't know,' she answered. 'He didn't give me any reason for refusing the loan. He simply said he didn't want it.'

'And then what?'

The color had returned to Gay's face and she seemed considerably more at ease.

'George asked me where I had the money,' she said. 'When I told him that I had it here, in the house, he suggested that in view of things, it would be wiser and of course safer if I put it in the bank as quickly as possible.'

'What d'you mean, Ma'm ... in view o' things?'

'O-h, in view of what had happened.'

'Y'mean to Snediker?'

'Yes.'

'I see.'

'I decided to take it to the bank without further delay. While the man there ...'

150

'His name's Oliver, Jed Oliver.'

'Thank you. While Mr. Oliver was entering the deposit in my name, I asked him to change it.'

'Change what, Ma'm?'

'I asked him to credit it to George's account.'

'Even though George didn't want it?'

'Yes.'

'Wa-al,' the Sheriff said. 'That sounds reas'nable t' me. Mind if I ask you somethin', Missus Hollis?'

'W-hy, no, of course not.'

'Where'd you get that money?'

'From my husband,' Gay explained gently. 'It was the money I got for our place in Texas.'

Loomis nodded understandingly. He turned toward the door, stopped, and looked at Cathy.

'Sure sorry I spoiled your supper,' he said with an apologetic smile.

'It isn't spoiled. I can heat things up again.'

'G'night,' Loomis called over his shoulder.

McCabe opened the door and went out. Cathy followed the Sheriff outside. She returned a minute later, closed the door, turned and stopped. Gay had gone. George followed Cathy's questioning eyes.

'She went upstairs,' he said. 'Mebbe you better go up too and see that she's awright.'

He turned, watched Cathy go up the stairs

151

... he heard a door on the upper floor open and close. He was motionless for a moment, then he got to his feet; he looked about the room, spied his hat lying on a far corner chair, strode over, caught it up, clapped it on his head and stalked out. The door swung wide, slammed shut behind him.

It was probably five minutes later when Cathy returned. She did not appear surprised to find that George had left the house. Slowly she began to clear the table. She paused once, and raised her head ... there was a curious tightness in her eyes and on her lips. She shook her head sadly, carried an armful of dishes away.

CHAPTER TEN

TIME AND TIDE

Early the next morning Phil Martin was buried in the fenced-off clearing on the fringe of the grove of tall cottonwood trees beyond the big house.

Cy Phillips ... the townsmen referred to him as 'Old Doc', and who combined a barbering business with the more serious activities and demands of an undertaker, a curious but not unusual thing in most small western towns ... had prepared the body for

152

burial the previous night. Four husky punchers carried the heavy coffin out of the cottage and hoisted it with a great deal of effort onto a sturdy farm wagon. Nettie Martin, black-clad, but firmly erect, emerged and fell in directly behind the wagon. The winded punchers trudged along behind her.

It was a strange morning for a funeral; the air was brisk and invigorating and life-giving, the limitless sky was a vast canopy of soft velvety blue with a batch of tiny white fleecy clouds hovering about, the sun was warm, happy and cheery. The grass underfoot had never seemed so richly alive, so brilliantly green and lush. George and Cathy joined Nettie on one side of the already dug grave. The coffin was unloaded and placed beside it. The punchers stood on the opposite side. Gay, her head bowed, stood behind the punchers. Ropes were slung under the coffin. Cathy nudged George and he turned to her.

'Say something,' she whispered. 'You must.'

He frowned, moistened his lips with his tongue, drew a deep breath. He raised his head.

'God,' he said aloud and somewhere among the tightly-grouped body of men facing him a man coughed lightly. 'God,' he said again. 'This is Phil Martin we're burying. He was a good man. We, his wife and his friends, ask you to take good care of him. Amen.'

George flushed as he finished. He gestured and four men stepped forward, gripped the ropes and lowered the coffin into the waiting grave. The ropes were jerked away, dropped on the ground and the four men returned to their original places; two others, with shovels clutched in their hands, came forward now, drove the shovels into the heaped dirt. As the first shovelful thudded on the coffin, Nettie flinched. Cathy stepped up to her quickly, put her arm around Nettie's waist. Presently the grave was filled and the dirt over it was smoothed down. There was a moment's silence, a motionless pause, then the punchers nearest the grave gathered up the ropes and the shovels. Finally the entire group of men, turning as one, tramped off. Gay moved away with them, quickened her pace and left them behind her, and fled in the direction of the house. Nettie, turning, followed her with her eyes. George came forward now. He halted at Nettie's side.

'Nettie,' he said and she looked up at him. 'Nettie, there ain't much anybody c'n say t' you at a time like this. Still, I want you t' know that I'm sorry.'

'Thank you,' she said with a quiet smile and he marvelled at her courage. 'And thank you for what you said about Phil. I know he would have liked it.'

He smiled at her in reply, fleetingly, boyishly and a bit embarrassedly.

154

'I don't know what plans you've made,' he went on. 'But I'd kinda like t' have you stay here. The cottage was home t' you and Phil, and even though he's gone now, I kinda think he'd like t' know you're still around.'

Tears welled up into her eyes.

'Thank you again,' she replied. 'I had hoped you would let me stay here, even if it was for only a little while. I ... I've got to get used to things now, that is, doing them alone, and it'll take a little time changing over. It'll be so much easier doing that here than anywhere else.'

He nodded vigorously, understandingly.

''Course,' he said.

'And you'll come to the house for your meals,' Cathy added. 'You won't be so alone then.'

Nettie's eyes turned toward the house.

'No,' she said quietly. 'I ... I'd rather not, if you don't mind.'

Cathy and George looked at each other, but neither pressed the point.

'And now,' Nettie said. 'I'd like to stay here for a while.'

'Of course,' Cathy said.

They left Nettie standing beside the grave. Minutes later, when they looked back, Nettie was on her knees. They trudged along in silence until they reached the house.

'That was sweet of you, George,' Cathy said.

He stopped, looked down at her, patted her shoulder, then he stepped past her and strode off toward the corral.

Gay was standing at the window in their bedroom when Cathy entered. Gay did not turn. Cathy stood beside her for a moment.

'When is she leaving?' Gay asked presently.

'She isn't leaving,' Cathy answered.

Gay looked at her quickly.

'George asked her to stay,' Cathy went on. 'I think it was the only decent thing to do. She accepted.'

There was no comment from Gay.

'It really shouldn't make any difference to you,' Cathy said. 'No more than it did before.'

'I don't like that woman,' Gay said finally.

'That's silly. You can't possibly have any real reason for disliking her.'

'But I do anyway. There ... there's something about her, the way she looks at me, that annoys me. Her eyes seem to bore into me.'

'I've never noticed that.'

'I have,' Gay persisted.

Cathy was silent for a moment.

'I think it's just your imagination, Gay,' she said. 'Unless, of course...'

'Unless what?'

'Nothing.'

'You were going to say that perhaps it was because of Phil ... weren't you?'

156

Gay turned to face her sister. Their eyes met.

'You were thinking that, weren't you, Cathy?'

'Yes,' Cathy admitted.

Gay came away from the window. She sauntered over to the bed, seated herself on the edge.

'Cathy,' Gay said and Cathy turned toward her again. 'Phil was in love with me. You didn't know that, did you?'

'N-o,' Cathy said. 'I didn't actually know it even though I did feel that there was something between you two.'

'What do you mean?'

'We-ll, it was after you returned from that night in the shack. I noticed that George wasn't so cordial toward you after that, then I began to suspect that perhaps everything wasn't just the way it was supposed to appear, or at least the way George said it was. I knew you'd never cared much for George. You said as much once. So it had to be Phil.'

'I see.'

'Do you think Nettie suspected anything?'

Gay shrugged a slender shoulder.

'I don't know,' she answered. 'However, I've had an idea for some time now that she suspected something but that she wasn't quite sure.'

'Perhaps that's why she looked at you so. Or perhaps that's why you imagined she looked at you,' Cathy said. 'I wonder if Phil ever told her anything?'

'I don't think so.' She got to her feet. 'Cathy, I'm going away.'

'But where will you go?'

'O-h, I'll find a place, never fear. It won't have to be much because anywhere at all will be better than staying here with her so near me. I couldn't stand that for long.'

'Perhaps it would be wisest.'

'Of course.'

'When do you plan to go?'

'The sooner the better. Probably tomorrow,' Gay said. 'Right now I think I'll go for a ride. The air and the exercise will do me good.'

Cathy followed her to the door.

'You'll be back for dinner, won't you?' she asked.

'I really don't know. The way I feel now, food doesn't sound particularly appealing. However, maybe after I've been out for a while, I'll feel differently. But don't worry about me. I'll be all right.'

★　　★　　★

It was early afternoon when Gay rode out of a concealing cluster of sun-bleached boulders and halted atop a sharp rise. Below her lay the open range, spreading away as far as the eye could see in a tremendously long and uneven series of rumpled grassy stretches of green carpeting. In the distance the sky seemed to meet the range, with nothing between them to indicate space.

She was tired now; she had ridden for hours without stopping. She had started off in an easterly direction, but now she discovered that she was riding steadily southward instead. Somewhere below her was the shack ... her eyes ranged over the open country but it seemed to have disappeared, lost in that great vastness. She winced inwardly when she thought of it, even tried to put the mental picture she had of it out of her mind, but it was wasted effort; there was something magnetic about the shack and despite her efforts to withstand it, she knew that eventually she would head directly for it. There was something else that disturbed her, although at the moment she seemed to have forgotten about it, just as she had forgotten about it before only to have it return to plague her. Once, when she had looked back, she had had the feeling that she had caught a fleeting glimpse of a rider some distance behind her. She had looked back a dozen times afterward, but even though she had seen nothing to confirm her suspicions, the feeling that she was being followed persisted.

She nudged her horse and he started downhill. The grassy slope was slippery, as he quickly discovered, and once or twice he barely managed to check himself in time to save both himself and Gay from a bad spill. From then on he went on with the utmost caution. There were some grassless stretches of ground and he sought them out whenever it was possible. But finally they reached level ground again. With a snort of mingled satisfaction and triumph, Gay's horse loped away. At times the thick lush grass completely muffled his hoof beats; at other times, when they clattered over isolated stretches of barren ground, his iron shoes rang out sharply and echoed for miles. Then she spied the shack, standing so completely alone on the range. She slowed her horse to a walk, halted him a dozen feet from it.

It looked so drab and uninviting in the broad daylight, yet so much had happened within the limited confines of its walls. She shook her head. Bits of events and flashes of familiar faces darted in and out of her thoughts. She was jolted back to reality when a slender figure suddenly came around the shack. It was Nettie Martin. Gay stared hard at her. Nettie stopped in front of her, looked up at her.

'I had a feeling that you'd come out here,' Nettie said.

Gay did not answer. Casually, Nettie reached up, patted the neck of Gay's horse, then just as casually, or so she evidently wanted it to appear, her hand came down a bit, encircled the rein and tightened around it.

'Funny, isn't it,' Nettie mused, 'that both of us should head for this miserable-looking place?'

'You were following me,' Gay said severely.

'I wondered if you knew,' Nettie said calmly. 'I circled around you and managed to get here half an hour ago and simply waited. I was so certain that you'd come, and you see, I was right, for here you are.'

'I didn't come here intentionally,' Gay flared up. 'I've been riding around for hours, as you know, and it was just a coincidence that I happened to ride this way. But thank goodness this will be the last time. I'm leaving the Circle-A.'

Nettie's eyes glinted.

'Going to hunt elsewhere for more scalps to add to your collection?' she asked sarcastically. 'Or should I have said more weak men's lives instead of just their heads?'

Gay flushed but she held her tongue.

Nettie studied her for a moment, eying her critically and appraisingly.

'So you're running away,' she mused finally. 'Yes, that would be what you'd do. But it won't help you any, Gay. You can't run away from the things you've done and expect to be able to forget them just by changing the scenery and substituting other men for the ones you've left behind you, even the dead

161

ones. Your conscience won't let you. It has a voice, you know, and even though you may try to muffle it, even choke it, somehow it will make itself heard. It'll keep pounding away at you, in your ears, in your heart, and you'll have to listen to it. Then it will get you. It never fails.'

Gay stiffened in her saddle ... she was indignant now and she raised her head, looked past Nettie as though Nettie wasn't there. Nettie disregarded it.

'You're a coward, Gay,' she continued. 'You haven't any morals or any principles, and you haven't the courage to do anything about it. You won't let yourself feel that you've done anything wrong. You won't let yourself feel any responsibility for anything, either. Maybe you didn't actually encourage Phil to fall in love with you. Maybe you didn't encourage the others either, and I'm sure there were others beside Phil, just as I'm sure there'll be others after him. All right, perhaps you didn't encourage them, but by the same token you didn't discourage them. You didn't, Gay, because you didn't have the decency or the courage. You're just as weak in your own way as Phil and the others were in their way.'

Gay's chin trembled, and her head came down. She sobbed softly. Nettie eyed her and frowned.

'Stop snivelling,' she commanded. 'Those

tears of yours don't come from the heart and they don't impress me at all. I want to know something. Did you know that Phil planned to kill himself?'

Gay sobbed even louder.

'You must have known,' Nettie went on. 'I didn't. I wouldn't be expected to know. After all, I was only his wife. It's odd, isn't it, how little a woman ever knows about her own husband, and how much more a woman like you, a woman who does nothing for him, knows about him? That's the ironic part of life, I suppose. O-h, for Heaven's sake ... stop crying!'

'I won't!'

'All right then ... don't!' Nettie snapped. 'You've probably resorted to tears and hysterics all your life in order to get out of things. They're your only weapons. But they don't mean a thing to me. I can see through them just as I can see through you. And do you know what I can see?'

'No!' Gay sobbed. 'And I don't care!'

'You're vain and self-centered and inconsiderate of everyone else. On top of that you're unprincipled as I said before. All in all, Gay, you're a sorry picture of a woman. And I'm really sorry for you. You'll never get any lasting happiness out of life. You don't deserve any.'

Nettie paused now. She looked tired and worn and her face was streaked and old. She drew a deep breath.

'I had planned to kill you, Gay,' she said presently. 'I brought a gun with me for that purpose. It wasn't just for the sake of revenge. I wanted to make sure you'd never be able to do to other women what you've done to me. But now I realize how foolish it was of me even to think of killing you. I should have known better. I'm a woman, born to give life, not to take away life. I think you'd better turn around now and go back home. I don't want to quarrel with you any longer. I . . . I don't feel up to it.'

Gay raised her head . . . in that instant her sobbing ceased completely and curiously enough, left no trace behind. She eyed Nettie strangely as though she didn't fully understand. Obviously she had expected the very worst, perhaps something physical in the way of punishment . . . now that she appeared to have gotten off so completely she seemed unable to take advantage of the situation.

'Go . . . please!'

Nettie released the reins. She stepped back a bit to give Gay's horse clearance. Slowly Gay wheeled her mount. She twisted around in the saddle, stared at Nettie.

'Go!' Nettie screamed.

She swung her right hand wildly, whacked the animal on the rump. He snorted angrily and bolted away.

Minutes later, when the thundering echo of

the horse's hoofs had died out, Nettie turned. Alone, her resolve and high determination vanished, and left her a broken and bowed woman. She was sobbing now, softly and gently, and her tears blinded her, caused her to stumble. A horse poked his head around the side of the shack ... he eyed her for a moment wonderingly, cocked his head to one side as he looked at her. He ambled forward now, the empty stirrup on the saddle on his back grazed the building ... he stopped in front of her. She collided with him ... he whinnied softly and she thrust out her arms, caught him around the neck. Her crying grew louder and she clung to him for support and when it seemed that her heart would break, she buried her face in his mane.

$$\star \qquad \star \qquad \star$$

It was three days since Gay had left the ranch, three long, drawn-out days that seemed never-ending to Cathy who had hoped with each new day's arrival for some word from her sister. Gay's failure to communicate with her weighed heavily on Cathy who went about her household duties silently. The house itself reflected her worry. It was hushed and shadowy and it seemed to be full of faint echoes of bygone sounds and steps and voices. It was to be expected that George would notice it ... he did and he looked at

Cathy and he opened his mouth as though to say something only to reconsider, then each time he frowned, clamped his jaws shut and stalked off.

Phil Martin's sudden death had left the ranch shaken and dazed ... when all conjecture over his unexplained death was over and no satisfactory conclusion had been arrived at, everyone lapsed into thoughtful silence. But now that Phil was buried, things quickly returned to normalcy. One marvelled at it, and of course seemed a bit taken back at the discovery that the things he had done and supervised could go on without him. It left one feeling badly, but even that sensation vanished in due course. Life, one quickly discovered, belonged to the living, and it was in a measure a tribute to them that they could make the necessary adjustments needed to continue their lives.

It was to be expected that Nettie Martin would be the last one to respond to this return to normalcy. She did not contradict the theory ... passers-by noticed that the blinds were drawn to their fullest over the cottage windows and they accepted it as natural that Nettie's grief should force her to attempt to erect a barrier between herself and the outside world. Yet, as the days went by and the blinds did not go up, few seemed to notice it. Perhaps interest in the dead had waned; perhaps it was due to the fact that the living were too concerned with matters pertaining to life and the living to notice it.

It was the evening of the third day. George came downstairs, sauntered to the table, swung his chair around and seated himself. Cathy placed a well-filled plate in front of him.

'H'm,' he said, eying it. 'That sure looks good.'

She turned away, returned presently with her own supper, put it down on the table, sat down opposite him.

'George,' she said and he looked up. 'I've heard from Gay.'

'That so?'

'Yes,' Cathy went on. 'She's taken a room in town, at Mrs. Sutton's place, a sort of boarding house.'

He wondered what else she would have to tell him ... he had already learned of Gay's new home, wondered if Cathy knew as he did that Gay had gotten herself a job as Corbin's cashier.

'Now I can see her whenever I want to,' Cathy continued. 'And she can come and visit us.'

' 'Course,' he said.

He picked up his fork. There was a knock on the door, and they looked at each other. He frowned, put down the fork, but Cathy was on her feet already ... she went to the door, opened it. In the open doorway stood a tall figure, Sheriff Buck Loomis. Behind him, and peering in over his shoulder was Pat McCabe. The frown on George's face deepened.

'You back again?' he said curtly.

Loomis pushed into the kitchen. He glanced at Cathy only briefly, and came forward to the table. He halted in front of it presently, and his right hand dropped to the butt of his gun. George's eyes followed Buck's hand ... now they came up again to meet the lawman's.

'Akers,' the Sheriff began with a curious heaviness in his voice. George heard the door close behind McCabe but he did not turn his head. 'Pat's just come back fr'm a trip down t' Texas.'

'Fr'm Shannon, Texas,' McCabe added.

'That's the town Cathy's sister was livin' in,' Buck went on, 'b'fore she come back here. Anyway, I had Pat check with the Sheriff there and a couple o' others includin' the feller that runs the bank in Shannon. Seems like Gay's husband, a feller named Dave Hollis, left 'er a small ranch and some dough.'

'Go on,' George said.

'I am,' Loomis said. He moistened his lips with a quick darting movement of his tongue. 'The ranch ain't been sold yet, so Gay didn't get 'ny dough outta that. The dough in the bank come to seventeen hundred dollars.'

168

Cathy came around the table. She halted behind her own chair.

'Then the five thousand dollars,' she said and she stopped abruptly when the full impact of what the Sheriff was leading up to struck her.

Loomis shook his head.

'It wasn't her money,' he said quietly. He looked down at George. 'I'm sorry, Akers, but you'll hafta come back t' town with us. You're under arrest f'r the murder o' John Snediker.'

CHAPTER ELEVEN

CORBIN SHOWS HIS HAND

Ted Corbin smiled the smile of a man who is pleased with things. It was an expansive smile and a stranger eying him for the first time would doubtless have been deceived by the Corbin smile and attributed to him all the virtues that began with tolerance and patience and Ted Corbin was neither tolerant nor patient. Ever since he could remember, the Corbin credo had been one of taking what a Corbin wanted and when a Corbin wanted it. Deliberating, planning ... they were the signs of a weak, timid man, hence a Corbin scorned such things. Patience was therefore something a Corbin refused to have linked with his name. As for tolerance, the Corbins had never heard of the word. The Corbins 'abided' certain people who possessed eye-arresting strength, either personal or commanded, and when the opportunity presented itself, turned upon that imposing yet momentarily unsuspecting and unwary worthy and struck him down. That lull in hostilities was the nearest approach to patience that the Corbins ever knew.

This night Ted Corbin was particularly pleased with things even though he had had no part in creating this pleasant situation. He was gloating over the fact that George Akers was languishing behind bars in the back room of the Sheriff's office. He had never forgotten the beating he had received at the youth's hands, and now the knowledge that George was in serious trouble gave him a tremendous sense of satisfaction. But the fact that he had but to raise his head to see the sky . . . it was a blue sky . . . despite his smile he was annoyed and the longer he reflected, the more annoyed he became. What, he asked himself, could he do to increase the depth of Akers' difficulties?

From where he stood in the open doorway of his place he had to raise his head to see the sky . . . it was a blue sky, and the bright moon and the sprinkling of twinkling, silvery stars overhead made a pretty picture. When a man is pleased even the elements must be at their best, and this night nature appeared to have outdone itself.

There was still another reason for the smile on Corbin's face. This was a purely personal reason and every now and then Corbin turned his head and looked inside, eyed Gay behind the cash counter, and the smile on his face deepened. Women had always occupied positions of importance in the lives of the Corbin men-folk and Ted was no exception. He was certain of one thing and that was that no Corbin had ever had as pretty a woman as Gay in his grasp. He had coveted Gay from the very first time he had seen her ... now, without any effort on his part, she was his. Life, indeed, he mused, could be wonderful ... and for the moment it was. A man stopped in front of him, looked at him and waited for Ted to become aware of his presence. Corbin settled himself against the framework of the door, found the man standing in front of him.

'O-h,' Corbin said. 'Didn't see you come along, Dan.'

The man laughed.

'Wondered when you were gonna notice me,' he replied. 'Don't know that I ever saw you lookin' so doggoned pleased with y'self, Ted.'

Corbin grinned broadly.

'Know who they got locked up down at the Sheriff's place?' he asked.

'Yeah, sure,' Dan said quickly. 'Tex Akers' boy.'

Corbin nodded grimly.

'He ain't been a boy f'r a long time,' he said curtly. 'He's a no-good killer, that's what he is.'

'Understand Buck Loomis got 'im dead t' rights. That right?' Dan asked.

'There was nothing to it,' Corbin asserted. 'Akers needed dough and he needed it pronto. When Snediker made 'im 'n offer f'r some o' his cattle, Akers turned it down. Why? Only because he had another way o' gettin' Snediker's dough and without havin' to give up a single head o' his cattle. He made out like Snediker wasn't offerin' him enough, then when Snediker left, this young polecat hustled away, circled around John, waylaid him and killed him. That's all there was to it. It was an open-and-shut case if ever I heard o' one, and Buck snapped it shut right smack in Akers' face.'

'I didn't have the hull story.'

'You have it now,' Corbin said grimly. 'Like I said b'fore, Akers is low-down, like a snake. And I know I don't hafta tell you what t' do with a snake, Dan.'

'Kill 'im right off.'

'Right.'

'Wa-al, the law'll fix 'im.'

'Yeah, sure, but that costs money, your money and mine. It costs real dough t' put on a trial and taxes are doggoned high as they are without addin' to 'em.'

'But we gotta give 'im a trial, don't we?'

Corbin scoffed openly.

'Akers killed Snediker just as sure as you an' me are standin' here,' he persisted. 'And nobody'll ever be able to tell me different. Then why'n hell should the county hafta pay out good money t' hang Akers when it could be done f'r nothing, huh?'

'You got somethin' there, Ted. Somethin' worth thinkin' about, too.'

Corbin straightened up so suddenly that Dan jerked back.

'Listen t' me,' Corbin said. Dan relaxed. 'I went outa my way one day t' try and do that young polecat a good turn. I didn't hafta do it, but I did anyway. I figgered he was up against it same as ol' Tex was, so I rode out t' the Circle-A and started t' make him an offer f'r the spread. Y'know what thanks I got?'

'Nope.'

'That young squirt told me t' get the hell off the place and t' stay off.'

Dan's eyes widened in surprise.

'On the level?'

Corbin nodded gravely.

'I'm tellin' you, Dan. 'Course you know I coulda grabbed him and busted him in two, but I didn't. I felt kinda sorry for 'im, so I just said, "if that's the way you want it, boy, it's awright with me". I got on my horse and rode away. But that oughta give you 'n idea o' what he's like. Pure cussedness. Now, c'n you blame me f'r feelin' about him the way I do?'

'Hell no!'

Corbin clapped him on the back.

'Go on inside, Dan,' he said, 'and tell Murphy I said to set up a bottle f'r you.'

Dan Caldwell brightened.

'Gee, Ted, that's swell o' you. Thanks, feller.'

'Forget it.'

Corbin watched him stride in, saw him head directly for the bar . . . after a minute he sauntered inside, too. He stopped at the counter. Gay looked up. Corbin smiled down at her.

'Know what time it is, young lady?' he asked.

'Wh-y, no. Is it . . . is it very late?'

'Nearly ten,' Corbin answered. 'Get your coat. You're going home. Think I want you t' get the wrong impression o' me, 'specially on your first night?'

Gay laughed softly.

'I love it here. It's so exciting.'

He nodded understandingly.

'I figgered you'd like workin' here. That's why I gave you the job,' he said. 'How was supper? Everything the way you wanted it?'

'Everything was delicious. I . . . I couldn't eat it all, though,' she replied. 'Thank you for looking out for me.'

He patted her cheek.

'Go get your coat. I'll wait for you outside.'

When she emerged minutes later Corbin came at once to her side. The street was dark and quiet. They started away at a brisk pace. When a shadow seemed to reach out at her from within a darkened doorway, Gay gasped, and Corbin quickly put a protecting arm around her, and guided her on. They neared the corner presently, stopped when a drunken man came reeling in their direction. Corbin, alert as before, promptly stepped in front of her and the drunk, staggering up to him, halted and looked up at him.

'Wa-al?' Corbin demanded.

The man evidently recognized him, or else the Corbin bulk which loomed up even bigger in the distorting darkness, cautioned him to exercise care and judgement ... at any rate he side-stepped with surprising nimbleness, circled around them hastily and they went on their way again. Mrs. Sutton's boarding house was located on the next block. They walked in silence, stopped when they reached the white-painted gate in front of the house.

'H'm,' Corbin muttered. 'Not a light lit in the hull danged house. What d'they do ... turn in at sundown? Come on.'

Gay caught his arm.

'Around the back,' she said. 'The kitchen door's unlatched.'

'Oh,' he said. He took her arm again, led her along a dark shadowy path that led to the rear.

'Beautiful out, ain't it?' he asked, nodding skyward. 'Moon and everything.'

'Sh-h-!' Gay cautioned him. 'Everyone's asleep.'

'The heck with th'm!' he whispered in her ear. 'They're too old t' appreciate a night like this.'

'It is beautiful,' she whispered in reply.

'Ordered it just f'r you,' he said.

There was a tall, thick trunked, full-limbed tree behind the house. It cast deep black shadows on the ground below. They stopped within a few feet of the kitchen door. Gay smiled up at Corbin.

'I've got to go in now,' she said in a low tone.

'Sure,' he said. She knew he would kiss her and she was not at all surprised when his big hands came up, tightened on her arms. Slowly he drew her to him. She did not resist him. He caught her in his arms, crushed her to him, bent his head and kissed her on the mouth.

'Mr. Corbin!' she breathed.

'Ted!' he corrected, and he kissed her again.

'Ted, please,' she whispered, squirming in his arms. 'You ... you mustn't!'

'Why not?'

'Someone may come out.'

He laughed softly.

'They better not!' he said. He kissed her again, loudly, hungrily. The kitchen door creaked open and Gay burst out of his arms, stepped away from him. 'Damn!' he said aloud.

'We lock the door for the night at ten o'clock, Mrs. Hollis,' a woman's voice said from the darkness behind the open door. 'Come in, please.'

Gay flashed past Corbin, and the door closed behind her. A key grated in the lock and a bolt was driven into place. Corbin tugged viciously at his pants belt, jerked it up a bit.

'Of all the nights,' he muttered angrily. 'This is the night this has t' happen t' me. An' just as I was...'

He turned and his voice trailed away. He stalked off, swung around the house, followed the path to the front of the house, glared at the darkened building, and stormed down the street. He was some fifty feet from the house when he heard approaching hoof beats. He swerved to the side of the street, stopped and looked up ... a horseman, shadowy and indistinct in the distance, loomed up. Presently the rider slowed his mount, clattered abreast of Corbin, then rode past him.

'A woman!' Corbin said half aloud. 'An' if

that wasn't Cathy Ballard, I'm plumb loco. Now what d'you s'ppose she's doin' here at this time o' night?'

He turned quickly, saw Cathy pull up in front of the boarding house, saw her dismount ... when he saw her trudge off toward the rear, he dashed back, came panting up to her waiting horse. He slipped down the length of the shadowy path, reached the end of it, jerked to a hasty stop and flattened out against the protective side of the house when he heard voices.

'I know it's terribly late, Mrs. Sutton,' he heard Cathy say. 'And you know I wouldn't think of disturbing you if it wasn't necessary. I simply must see my sister.'

'We-ll,' Mrs. Sutton's voice said. 'Come in. Her room is at the head of the stairs, to the right. I'm going back to bed. You might tell your sister to let you out when you go, and to be sure to lock up!'

'I will,' Cathy answered. 'And thank you.'

Corbin heard the door close, but this time the key did not grate in the lock, nor did the bolt rasp home. He smiled grimly, slipped around to the door, listened at it for a moment, then he turned the knob gently. The door opened and he peered inside. The lower floor was dark ... he raised his head, spied a tiny light on the upper floor. He stepped inside, closed the door behind him, tiptoed to the stairway, drew a deep breath, then he went up the stairs. Presently he reached the landing.

'To the right,' he muttered, and turned in that direction. The light was directly overhead in a tiny swinging ceiling lamp. He stopped, eyed it, reached up, and with a single twist of his wrist turned down the wick, plunging the upper floor into total darkness. He had already noted the door. Now he inched his way up to it, knelt down at the keyhole, put his ear to it.

'Gay,' he heard Cathy say. 'I came here to ask you something and I won't go 'till you tell me what I want to know.'

'O-h, Cathy, for heaven's sake,' Gay replied. 'I've had a long day and now I'm terribly tired.'

'Don't you think I'm tired, too?' Cathy countered. 'I want to know where you got the five thousand dollars you offered first to lend George and later deposited to his credit in the bank.'

'O-h, that?' Gay asked with a drawn-out yawn. 'You heard me tell the Sheriff, didn't you?'

'That you got it from Dave? Yes.'

'Then for goodness sake...'

'But you didn't get it from Dave,' Corbin heard Cathy say.

'I didn't mean that Dave actually gave it to me,' Gay said quickly. 'What I meant was that that was money I got for selling the ranch

179

after Dave died. Now do you understand?'

'I don't know yet. Who'd you sell the ranch to?'

'O-h, some man.'

'What was his name?'

'His name?' Gay repeated. 'Let me see now.'

There was a brief silence in the room.

'Well?' Cathy asked presently.

'I'm afraid I've forgotten it,' Gay said. 'I'll probably remember it the minute you've gone. But his name isn't important now, is it?'

'How much did you get for the ranch?' Cathy asked, disregarding her sister's question.

'O-h, sixty-five hundred dollars, I think it was.'

'Don't you know?'

'You know how I am about such things, Cathy. They don't mean very much to me.'

'Evidently. Who sold the ranch for you, Gay? The bank?' Cathy asked.

'Of course,' Gay said. 'I wouldn't have known what to do by myself.'

'The bank people gave you a copy of the bill of sale, didn't they?'

'They gave me something.'

'That's more like it. By the way, where do you keep it, that something the bank gave you?'

'O-h, it's somewhere around.'

'Probably in your trunk.'

'Yes, that's where it is.'

'Would you mind getting it out, please?' Cathy asked. 'Or better still, since you're so tired, if you'll give me the key, I'll get it.'

'Now that I think of it,' Gay said hastily, 'it isn't in the trunk. I wonder where it was that I saw it last? I'll have to think about it, Cathy. But it'll come to me, never fear.'

There seemed to be some sort of movement within the room . . . when Cathy spoke again Corbin decided that she had moved.

'Gay,' she said with finality, 'I think this has gone far enough. Everything you've told me is a lie, and you know it. What's more, the Sheriff knows it, too. He sent his deputy, that red-headed McCabe man, down to Shannon, and he knows all there is to know. The bank hasn't sold the ranch, so it isn't at all surprising that you couldn't think of the name of the man who bought it. There wasn't five thousand dollars in Dave's account, either. There was only seventeen hundred. Those are just two of the things the Sheriff mentioned. What the others are, and I suppose there must be others, I don't know. But they don't interest me at the moment.'

There was a pause, a deep, heavy stillness behind the closed door . . . Corbin pressed his ear closer to the keyhole.

'Gay,' he heard Cathy say, 'this is serious. Actually it's a matter of life and death. Can

181

you understand that? George has been arrested for the murder of John Snediker and the only link between George and the killing is that five thousand dollars. I know he didn't kill that man. But that isn't enough. If we could prove that the money was yours, or that you got it from someone else, someone other than George, then the Sheriff wouldn't be able to hold George for a minute...'

Gay was tight-lipped.

'For the last time, Gay, will you tell me where you got that money?'

'I ... I can't tell you.'

'Did you get it from George?' Cathy pressed her.

'Cathy, please...'

'Did you?'

'I won't tell you!'

'Gay, this may mean George's life. I love him. You'd better tell me, do you hear?'

A sob broke from Gay.

'Did you get that money from George?' Cathy screamed.

'I won't tell you!' Gay cried.

Corbin swung around toward the stairway ... he expected Mrs. Sutton to come pounding up the stairs as a result of Cathy's scream. When he failed to hear a door open on the lower floor, he decided that Mrs. Sutton had fallen asleep, and he was relieved. He bent over the keyhole again.

'All right, Gay,' he heard Cathy say

heavily. 'I know how you got that money. You murdered Snediker. You're the one who'll hang. Think of it, Gay ... your pretty white neck in that coarse rope noose, your hands tied behind you. The rope will tighten and you'll scream. Someone will laugh and you'll scream even louder. The rope will tighten more, then more and more, and it'll choke you, stifle your last scream. It'll be awful, awful!'

'No!' Gay sobbed hysterically. 'No! I won't hang, I tell you ... I won't! I didn't kill Snediker! It was Phil, Phil Martin who did it. I know because he told me he did!'

'Then how did you get Snediker's money?' Cathy hurled at her relentlessly. 'How did you get it?'

'I got it from Phil,' Gay wailed brokenly.

'No one in the world will believe that.'

'Phil gave it to me!'

'You're lying again, Gay ... you're lying!'

There was a sudden rush of steps, as though one of the sisters had flashed across the room. Then Corbin understood it, even visualized it without seeing the actual position ... Gay, he told himself, had surrendered. She was in Cathy's arms, clinging to her, crying pitifully ... she made Corbin think of a child who caught in a falsehood, tries to brazen it out to the very end only to sense futility and turns from a hysterical defiance to complete capitulation.

'I took the money from Phil,' Gay sobbed.

'But you meant to return it, didn't you?' Cathy asked. She was pleading with Gay to show some decency. 'You meant to turn it over to the authorities, didn't you?'

'I don't know what I meant to do with it,' Corbin heard Gay whimper miserably.

'Was Phil still alive when you took the money from him?' Cathy asked her.

'No.'

'Why did he kill himself? He did kill himself, didn't he?'

'Yes,' Gay answered. 'He had begged me to go away with him. I'll never know why I agreed. It must have been because he was so terribly unhappy, and I was so sorry for him. Anyway, he killed Snediker in order to get money with which to finance our going away. When he told me what he had done, I was frantic. I remember telling him that I wanted no part of him, of the money. He tried to strike me, but I avoided him somehow, managed to get out of the shack. I was some distance away from it when I heard a shot. I ran back and looked in. Phil lay on the floor. He ... he was dead.'

'He killed himself because he wasn't strong enough to face the consequences,' Cathy said. 'When you escaped, that was the end of him. He must have sensed that your very first thought would be of the Sheriff and that was more than he could stand. So he chose what

184

he thought was the easiest way out.'

'I suppose so.'

'There was more than just the five thousand dollars, wasn't there?'

'Oh, yes ... Quite a lot more. It's in my trunk.'

'That's why you didn't want me to see what you had in there,' Cathy said quickly. 'Get your things on, Gay. We're going to call on Sheriff Loomis.'

'The Sheriff?' Gay repeated. There was fear in her voice.

'Yes,' Cathy said. 'If you're telling the truth, and I think you are now, you've nothing to fear. Hurry. It's getting late.'

A few minutes later the sisters emerged from Gay's bedroom. Corbin had already backed away from the door and into the protective darkness of a far corner. They groped their way to the stairs, went down the steps and out of the house. When he heard the back door close behind them, he moved swiftly, entered Gay's room. A lamp burned brightly atop a bureau that stood against one wall ... the trunk was just beyond it. The lock on the trunk was old ... it yielded without offering much resistance to Corbin's knife blade, and finally, to pressure from the barrel of his gun. Locating the balance of John Snediker's money was even easier ... Gay had concealed it in the folds of one of her petticoats. Corbin grinned broadly, pocketed the money, left the room without delay, made his way to the stairway, down the steps and finally to the back door. In another minute he was safely out of the house. In the enveloping darkness there was a grim smile on his face ... it was a reflection of a plot he was concocting.

CHAPTER TWELVE

TEX AKERS SLEEPS CONTENTEDLY

Corbin found his place well crowded when he returned. He looked about quickly, nodded when he noted in that sweeping glance that most of his friends were there. He noticed too that their faces were flushed, an indication that they had been doing plenty of drinking in his absence. He had hoped for that, and now he felt reassured for the success of his plot. There were some twenty men at the bar, and another eight or ten sitting at the tables. Dan Caldwell was at the far end of the bar with Nat Devine, a burly rancher ... they looked up when Corbin entered. Devine nudged Caldwell, whispered something to him and both men laughed.

'Sure took you a long time t' take the little lady home, Ted,' Devine said with a sly grin.

'Didn't it though?' Caldwell added. 'An'

it's on'y two short blocks to the boardin' house no matter which way you go.'

Sandy-haired Johnny Hewitt, Devine's foreman, stood on Caldwell's left. Devine nudged him and Hewitt nodded understandingly.

'Yeah,' he said. 'But what you fellers seem to've forgot is that that last block is darker'n all get-out, so mebbe they had t' stop every now and then t' kinda get their bearings. Y'know, that r'minds me o' the time Jake Flowers was courtin' that girl ... you fellers must r'member her ... the tall, lean, willowy blonde who came t' help out Jed down at the bank?'

'Heck, yes,' Devine said quickly. 'I don't r'member what her name was, but she was the one with the rollin' eyes an' the hips t' match, wasn't she?'

'Uh-huh,' Hewitt said with a nod. 'That's the one, awright. Anyway, it seems that Jake got 'imself quite a case on her, an' he started follerin' her around like a puppy dog. He hung around the bank like he was its on'y depositor.'

Murphy was plying a damp towel on the glistening surface of the bar. He looked up, chuckled in his toothless mouth.

'Huh,' he grunted. 'Jake never had more'n two bits in 'is life. He used t' pay f'r the first drink he'd order, but the second one allus went on the cuff. He was a character, awright.'

'So was his old man,' someone added.

'Gettin' back to Jake,' Hewitt continued, 'he took this girl home one evenin'.'

'Now that I think uv it, Johnny,' Devine interrupted, 'wasn't her name Flossy an' didn't she live at the boardin' house, too?'

'I wouldn't know,' Hewitt said dryly. 'I was never intr'duced to 'er, and what's more, I never took 'er home.'

'Go on with your story,' Caldwell said. 'You fellers shut up f'r a minute.'

'If that's supposed t' mean me,' Devine said, 'I'm plumb shut.'

'Wa-al,' Hewitt went on, 'it seems like Jake didn't show up f'r two hull days after startin' out with this Flossy. His ol' man fin'lly got tired o' waitin' f'r Jake t' come home an' fix breakfast so he up an' went out lookin' for Jake. I'm doggoned if it didn't take ol' Ben two days t' get back, too.'

There was a roar of laughter when Johnny finished.

'Ted's a helluva better man than either o' the Flowers,' Caldwell said presently. 'He made it back here the same danged night.'

Corbin grinned sheepishly, stepped up to the bar, then when he turned around the expression on his face had changed. Devine eyed him, circled around Caldwell and Hewitt, sauntered up to him.

'S'matter?' he asked. 'Can't you take a little

kiddin'?'

'You oughta know me better'n t' hafta ask a question like that,' Corbin replied.

'Then what are you lookin' so sore about?' Devine demanded. 'Somethin' wrong?'

Corbin nodded grimly.

'And how,' he said. He turned his head. 'Hey, one o' you fellers near the door ... close it, will yuh? Then all uv yah come over here. I've got somethin' t' tell you.'

A man arose from one of the tables, stepped to the door, slammed it shut, then, he hitched up his pants and followed some other table sitters toward the bar. They formed an uneven semicircle around Corbin. A couple of them were flushed, others were red-eyed and most of them were unsteady on their feet.

'You fellers all know me,' Corbin began. 'I ain't an angel and I don't pretend t' be one. Like you fellers, I like my liquor and I like my fun, when I know where t' draw the line.'

Nat Devine frowned.

'What'n hell are you talkin' about?' he demanded.

'You just keep listenin' f'r a minute,' Corbin retorted, 'and you'll find out. T'night I got wind o' the lousiest, dirtiest trick I ever heard tell uv, and soon's I heard uv it, I come hotfootin' it back here. I know who murdered John Snediker. Fact is, I know the hull stinkin' story behind it and it's made me

189

sick.'

One of the men facing him belched suddenly ... he reddened with embarrassment and Corbin glared at him.

'It musta been somethin' I ate,' the man said apologetically.

'I'll bet it was,' Corbin said coldly, then he turned toward the others. 'George Akers was b'hind the hull thing, him an' Gay Hollis.'

'O-h, yeah?' Devine said.

'Y'see,' Corbin added, 'George has been playin' around with Gay.'

Devine grinned slyly again.

'O-h, is that what's bitin' you?' he asked.

Corbin shook his head.

'Nope,' he said evenly. 'I ain't got 'ny claims on 'er so she c'n do all the playin' around she wants to. An' b'lieve me, she does. What's more, she don't draw the line nowheres. Maybe that don't sound compl'ment'ry t' me, but what the hell! Anyway, t' get back t' my story, it seems that Phil Martin fell f'r Gay, too. George knew about it but he didn't let it bother him none. Long's he got what he wanted, he was satisfied. If he'da raised hell with Gay about it, maybe she'da liked it better, but George was too smart t' let her know he was jealous.'

Murphy leaned over the bar, tapped Corbin on the shoulder ... Corbin turned his head slightly.

'How 'bout a drink, Boss?' the bartender

asked. 'You sound kinda dry.'

'Yeah,' Corbin said. 'I am dry. And set up a drink f'r the others, too.' There was a brief pause while Murphy poured the drinks ... they were downed in a single gulp and the glasses put down on the bar, then all attention was centered again on Corbin. 'Like everybody knows, George Akers was up against it for dough. You all know that John Snediker came t' him with 'n offer f'r some o' the Circle-A cattle and that Akers turned him down cold. F'r your inf'rmation, George woulda turned him down if he'da tripled his offer. Why? B'cause George had a scheme cooked up so's he could get all o' Snediker's dough without havin' t' give up a single head o' his cattle. What's more, nob'dy in the hull world would've known about it.'

'Hey,' Hewitt said admiringly. 'That's awright.'

'Ain't it though?' another man mused aloud.

'Shut up, you fellers,' Caldwell said thickly. 'Go on, Corbin. This is gettin' more interestin' all the time.'

'Martin's fallin' f'r her didn't mean anything special to Gay,' Corbin continued. 'He was just another man in her life and that was all. But Phil was plumb loco over 'er and the more he saw uv her, the more he wanted, till finally he couldn't stand it any more. He simply had t' have her, all uv 'er, too, and all

191

f'r 'imself. Gay ain't the kind t' be satisfied with one man, but she figgered that mebbe Phil could help her get away fr'm the Circle-A an' help her get to places where she could really do things for herself. She kinda hinted t' him that she wouldn't mind chuckin' over things f'r him, so that left Phil with a problem he hadn't figgered on. He'd hafta have dough, and a-plenty uv it, too. Like I said b'fore, Gay purposely told George everything that happened b'tween Phil an' her...'

'Everything?' Devine asked, grinning.

'Uh-huh,' Corbin said. 'Anyway, Phil didn't hafta look too long an' too far f'r ready cash. Along came Snediker wavin' a fistfull o' dough, and Phil's eyes popped. George noticed it and he figgered out what was goin' on in Phil's mind. He turned Snediker down cold, and you all know what happened. Snediker was found dead, murdered, and his dough was gone. Phil Martin killed him, miles away fr'm the Circle-A, grabbed Snediker's dough and went t' meet Gay. I dunno why he told her how an' where he got the dough, but he did, and even gave it t' her t' hold. The minute she got her hands on it, she beat it, leavin' Phil out in the cold. He couldn't take it, so he killed himself.'

'That's some story,' Devine said. 'And what happened t' the dough? How'd Akers get it?'

'You oughta be able t' figger that out f'r

y'self,' Corbin answered. 'Gay gave it t' George. Maybe that was the on'y way she could hold on to him. He took it, used it, and never said a single word. F'r my dough, he's the one responsible f'r Snediker's murder, not Martin. He was just a poor fool. Now what d'you s'ppose is gonna happen to George? He'll get away with a hull skin while Martin rots six feet under.'

'Akers oughta be strung up!' Caldwell said in his liquor-thickened voice.

'Damned right, he oughta!' someone else added.

'Wa-al,' Corbin said. 'Seems like we all feel the same way about it. The next thing is . . . what d'we do about it? I ain't the kind that helps elect a Sheriff one minute, and takes the law into my own hands the next minute, but there are times, like this f'r instance, when the law don't give me the satisfaction it oughta. And why? B'cause I know danged well that no matter what kind o' proof we c'n bring into court, Judge Scott'll turn it against us. You know same's I do that there ain't a lawyer in the hull West who can stand up t' the old Judge. Awright then . . . what d'we do about it?'

'Get a rope!' Caldwell yelled. 'And we'll damn soon show you what we'll do!'

'Here y'are,' Murphy said and he swung a coil of rope up from the floor and with the same motion slammed it down on the bar.

'Here's your rope, partner.'

Strong hands reached for it, and in a brief span of seconds thirty men with grim-faced Dan Caldwell leading them stormed out of the place, headed for the Sheriff's office down the street. Corbin followed them out ... in another minute he came back. Murphy looked up in surprise.

'S'matter?' he asked.

'You go with th'm,' Corbin said quickly. Murphy ripped off his apron, slung it aside, came swinging out from behind the bar. 'It'll look better if I kinda tag along toward the end o' things. Get it?'

'Yeah, sure. But s'ppose someb'dy asks what b'come o' you? What'll I tell 'em?'

'Just say quick-like that I'm lockin' up the cash and that I'll be along d'rectly. But don't let th'm hold things up f'r me.'

The pudgy bartender grinned significantly ... and evilly.

'Right,' he said and he went out, pulled the door shut behind him.

Corbin turned, strode to the cash drawer under the bar, opened it ... the door creaked and he raised his head. He stared hard for framed in the doorway was a tall, lean figure in whose big right hand a Colt gleamed menacingly and its muzzle seemed to gape at Corbin with hungry, ever-widening jaws. Corbin gulped. He saw George thrust his leg backward, heard the door slam shut, then as he stood rooted to the floor, George came up to the bar. The tall youth leaned over it suddenly, and he snatched Corbin's gun out of its holster, flipped it backward . . . it spun across the room, struck the far wall, caromed off, slid floorward until it collided with a table leg which stopped its wild flight.

'Awright,' George said curtly. 'Come outta there.'

Slowly Corbin closed the cash drawer; slowly too he turned and trudged the length of the bar, came out from behind it and stopped. George had followed him to the end of the bar; now, the Colt still steady in his right hand, he looked coldly at Corbin.

'I s'ppose,' he said evenly, 'I oughta tell you that Judge Scott, Sheriff Loomis and me heard everything you told them other fellers. I gotta hand it t' you, Corbin. You're just about the most c'nvincin' liar I ever heard. Y'know, f'r a minute, while I was listenin' t' you, I f'rgot I was the one you were lyin' about. I got so danged mad at me f'r doin' the things you said I did, I wanted t' beat hell outta me. Good thing I stopped myself. I s'ppose I oughta tell you that Mrs. Sutton saw you sneak outta her house, and that that was how we knew it was you who stole the rest o' Snediker's dough outta Gay's trunk. We worked our way around t' your back window, Corbin, and got into your storeroom, opened the door a crack and heard the hull show. It was pretty good, on'y we knew you were lyin' like hell and that kinda spoiled it f'r us.'

Corbin turned slightly and his eyes watched the door hopefully, eagerly ... George was motionless, silent, then Corbin suddenly jerked his head around. George grunted.

'No use hopin' f'r somethin' that can't happen,' he said gruffly. He holstered his gun, unbuckled his belt and took it off, turned on his heel and strode to the door. He opened it, tossed the belt into the street, turned again and came striding back. Corbin heard the door close gently. George stopped, picked up a chair and slung it across the room, caught up another and swung it over his head, then whirling, sent it spinning over the bar. The long wall mirror behind the bar and the double tier of whiskey bottles stacked in front of the mirror disintegrated with a shattering crash. A cry of rage preceded a bull-like rush by Corbin ... George tried to side-step but the burly Corbin, plunging at him like a pain-maddened steer, struck him and sent him spinning away. George crashed into a table and Corbin, swinging at him blindly, sent him reeling away. Blood flecked his lips and the sight of it seemed to enrage Corbin all the more ... he swarmed over George, breathing through his open mouth, smashing at him with his huge fists. George went down again and Corbin leaped on him but George twisted away in time as Corbin came crashing down on his hands and knees. George scrambled to his feet, backed away after casting a hasty glance backward to make certain there was nothing behind him. Corbin bellowed something indistinct and came plunging forward again, his heavy arms outthrust as though he sought to catch George in them and thus crush him in them.

George side-stepped nimbly, struck swiftly, and whirled away ... he came flashing forward again, struck twice more, hard, cutting blows, then he was away again. Corbin roared with rage, turned slowly, raised his arms again when George glided in and drove a murderous punch into Corbin's stomach, pivoted and with almost the same motion, lifted his same fist into Corbin's face. Blood spattered Corbin's shirt-front and he stopped, looked down at it ... George's fist came swinging through space and thudded cruelly against Corbin's nose with a curious, crunching sound. Again blood spurted from Corbin's face. He was panting now, open-mouthed, his head bent forward a bit, his heavy legs quivering. There were blood smears on his nose and mouth. He closed his mouth, doubled his fists, moved forward ... George met him. A hard punch that carried wrist-deep into Corbin's stomach doubled him up ... another punch that came whistling upward in an arching swing landed flush on his jaw and straightened him up and sent him staggering away on wobbly legs.

He fell against a table, forced himself upright again, moved away when George pursued him, and caught up with him near the door. Corbin folded his arms over his face but George hammered him relentlessly, gritted as he drove his punches home, concentrating for a minute on his burly opponent's body, then shifting to Corbin's head, rocking him with powerful smashes. Corbin's arms came down slowly and he sagged and fell sideways. George, panting heavily, checked himself and Corbin dragged himself to his feet. He came erect presently, turned to meet the onslaught ... George, pivoting on firmly planted feet, struck him twice more and Corbin fell like a poled steer, struck the floor on his battered face and rolled over on his back, his leaden arms outflung.

George stepped over him, opened the door ... a girl flung herself at him and he caught her in his arms.

'Are you ... all right?' Cathy asked him anxiously.

He grinned down at her.

''Course,' he said.

She peered at him closly.

'Bend down,' she commanded. He bent lower and she used her handkerchief to wipe away a thin trickle of blood at the corner of his mouth. 'It won't stop bleeding. We'll fix it up though when we get home.'

'Sure,' he said.

Two men came toward them ... Sheriff Loomis and a stocky man with white hair. Loomis eyed George for a moment, then he grinned at him.

'You don't look 'ny diff'rent,' he said finally. 'How about Corbin?'

'O-h, he ain't changed so much that you won't be able t' recog'nize him,' George answered. ''Course you'll hafta overlook some things, f'r instance like his teeth. Some o' them are scattered around. Then too his right eye's closed f'r r'pairs and the left one looks like a sunset.'

'Anything else?'

'The left side o' his face looks like he's havin' a heck uva time with mumps, but outside o' that...'

'Uh-huh,' Loomis said. 'He ain't changed much. Where did you leave the carcass?'

'Where it fell,' George replied. 'Just inside the door. Oh, yeah ... you'll probably find all that missin' Snediker dough in his pants pocket. It sure looked t' be full o' somethin'.'

The Sheriff turned, strode into Corbin's place.

'What become o' the mob?' George asked.

Judge Scott smiled.

'O-h, I intercepted them, with the aid of the Sheriff, of course,' he said. 'I pointed out the error of Corbin's ways, and suggested that they abandon their avowed determination to

199

hang you. And curiously enough, they accepted my suggestion without question, and dispersed and went home.'

'An' Gay?'

The Judge's face seemed to grow very grave.

'I made a suggestion to that young lady, too,' he replied. 'She's decided to seek other pastures. The Sheriff will see to it that she is safely settled on the first eastbound stage tomorrow morning. She felt that she would rather go westward, claimed there was far greater opportunity there, but I failed to agree with her.'

'I see,' George said.

'I've instructed the Sheriff to arrange transportation for her to Kansas City,' Judge Scott continued. 'I've a brother there, and he'll take her in hand. One of the things my brother will see to will be a weekly letter to Cathy.'

'Thank you,' Cathy said.

The Judge smiled at her, then he looked up at George again.

'We-ll, son,' he said. 'What now?'

'Reckon we'll head f'r home,' George answered. 'I'll be back here again t'morrow mornin' t' see what I c'n do with the bank about extendin' my note. It's due t'morrow, y'know.'

'I'll talk with Jed if you want me to.'

'I'd sure appreciate it, Judge, if you would.

He'll listen t' you ... I know that.'

'He usually does,' the Judge said in reply. 'However, I can't guarantee anything. You see, George, banks don't look upon single men as good risks. There's always the fear that a single man will clear out without a thought to his responsibilities. In your case, you might get the urge, even tomorrow morning, to return to your rodeo or perhaps the wanderlust will get you, and off to California you'll go.'

'I don't aim t' go anywheres but home,' George said with finality. 'There ain't any reason why the Circle-A shouldn't pay. Anyway, I'm gonna give it everything I got and I'm doggoned if I let a ranch beat me.'

'I admire your courage,' the Judge said. 'I'm still afraid Jed may insist upon two signatures on your note. Of course, I'll endorse it, so that leaves but one more signature to be obtained. Would Cathy endorse it, do you think? Assume your responsibility?'

'Wait a minute, Judge,' George said quickly. 'I ain't got any right t' ask Cathy t' do a thing like that.'

'If she were married to you, that would solve your difficulties in a jiffy. Incidentally, why don't you two get married?'

George gulped, flushed, averted his eyes.

'George is promised to someone else,' Cathy said evenly. 'Her name's Pat, and she's very pretty and she sings very beautifully, too.'

'I see,' Judge Scott said slowly.

George whirled upon Cathy.

'Who said I was promised t' her?' he demanded fiercely. 'Who did, huh?'

'We-ll, you didn't actually say so, but you certainly acted that way,' she retorted. 'You've mooned around like a lonesome, lovesick calf.'

'That so? If I did, doggone it, it wasn't my fault. I tried t' be nice t' you and where did it get me, huh? You didn't pay 'ny more attention t' me than . . .'

'Did you pay any attention to me?' she demanded. 'No, you didn't! All I was there for was to cook your meals, wash and darn your things, clean your house. That's how important I was to you! I might just as well have been an old Indian squaw for all you cared!'

Cathy was sobbing now, softly, and her head was bowed. The Judge turned his back. George looked down at her for a moment, raised his hands, lowered them, raised them again, and gripped her shoulders.

'Awright,' he said. 'I'm sorry. But stop cryin', will yuh? I . . . I can't stand it.'

She sniffed once or twice, but her crying did not stop.

'Hey,' he said and he shook her gently. 'Cathy, please.' Then he seemed to sense the

202

futility of reasoning with her in her present state ... he drew a deep breath, brought her close to him. He bent his head. 'Cathy, honey,' he whispered.

Judge Scott had turned around. Cathy had raised her head, and her sobbing had ceased completely.

'Will yuh?' the Judge heard George ask her.

'But what about Pat?'

'Doggone it, Cathy, can't you f'rget her?'

'Can you?'

'Would I be askin' you t' marry me if I couldn't?' George countered.

'We-ll,' Cathy said hesitantly.

Judge Scott coughed behind his upraised hand.

'Pardon me,' he said. 'I am returning to my office. If you should want me, that is both of you, you can find me there. Incidentally, I might mention that only one witness is required at a marriage ceremony.'

* * *

Judge Scott was sitting in his office, when they appeared there, his feet propped up on the edge of his desk. He insisted upon them remaining there while he went out in search of the witness the law required. It was ten minutes later when he returned, followed by a sheepishly grinning Sheriff Loomis who, hat in hand, was doing his best to slick back the few remaining hairs on his head.

'Buck,' the Judge said. 'You'll stand here. Cathy, please stay where you are. George, stand next to Cathy please. Take her hand, son.'

There was an impatient knock on the door, and red-headed Pat McCabe opened it and poked his head inside.

'Oh!' he said. 'Excuse me!'

'Wait up there,' Buck called. 'Want 'nything?'

Pat grinned.

'Got somethin' f'r Cathy,' he answered. 'I just ran into Mrs. Martin drivin' a hull wagon load o' stuff outta town. She said t' tell George that she was goin' back home after all. She gave me somethin' she said she'd found in the cottage when she was gettin' her own stuff t'gether. She said Cathy'd know what t' do with the thing and fr'm the looks o' things 'round here, it oughta come in handy right now. Here y'are, Cathy.'

Cathy came to him at once and he handed her something, turned on his heel and went out. They heard his step on the stairs. Cathy held something aloft ... it was a ring.

'George!' she said excitedly. 'Isn't it wonderful? It's my mother's wedding ring!'

Photoset, printed and bound in Great Britain by REDWOOD PRESS LIMITED, Melksham, Wiltshire

(X)-3-28-09